In Search of the Genuine

Through the Eyes of a Pilot, a Husband, and a Father

Richard E. Lee

To my wife and two sons

Contents

Preface

For years I've had loads of ideas for a book floating around in my head, all lacking a single focus. Eventually an idea came to me that cleared up all the indecision in an instant. I could write a book of short stories, well, sort of—chapters that were *short story-esque,* each different, but all loosely connected to each other. This is what I have endeavored to do.

Though many of the experiences are based around actual historical events, this book is fiction. The characters and settings are all of my own invention. Yet, they are handling real life situations, similar to what you may be up against. In that way this book is born out of truth.

These stories are about *searching for the genuine*— what really matters—through the eyes of one man, who is a pilot, a husband, and a father. This guy lives out his dreams in ways he thinks will bring meaning to his life. He raises a family and aims for the "good life." He faces career fallout after the 9-11 attacks and copes with life in a combat zone. Like all of us, his experiences are sometimes exciting and elating, and at other times they are downright disillusioning and disappointing.

Although this is not a religious book, it is about seeking and finding, losing and recovering. It's about having faith and latching on to a power greater than our own. It is my hope that you will enjoy the read, extract from it what you may need, and find some measure of truth about what is truly real and lasting in life.

The House

It was an exciting time of year—Christmas time. To add to the excitement, I had just been awarded a Captain position at my airline. After more than ten years of being a First Officer, I was finally reaching the peak of my career—becoming a major airline Captain. *Captain Richard Wellington Jr.* . . . wow, I liked the sound of that.

We lived in San Antonio, Texas. But soon we would strike our tent and move northeast, way northeast. I was to be based in Boston. However, we were not going to live in Boston but in Kittery, Maine, where my wife, Marie, had family. It was not going to be a bad commute at all from Maine down to Boston for my trips. Unlike most professions, when I go to work, I go away for several days. My drive down to Boston's Logan Airport would be made only four or five times a month.

I was certainly going to miss living in Texas, but this was something I just couldn't turn down. Our two sons, Richie and Jack, were both born in Texas, and we were quite comfortable with everything about living in the San Antonio area. But they were young and I knew they would adapt. I've never really cared for cold weather, but who cares? I was going to be a Captain! The raise in pay alone would be enough to get financing for the new *Captain's home!* At last, after squeaking through and juggling finances for years, we were finally going to live like an airline pilot and his family was supposed to live. An added bonus was the fact that Marie was excited about living near her family; this was all positive. Whoo-hoo! Life was good.

It all happened fast. Our house in Texas sold in three weeks, and I found myself in school learning the B737-200 in a matter of days after receiving the bid award. I had a printed copy of the bid award that I carried around in my pocket while at the training center. The training center— also known as "Stress U," "Tension Tech," and the "Schoolhouse"—was located in San Antonio, so I enjoyed going home every night for a change of pace. Things were hectic at the house though, as we were packing up for the move, and soon to close on the sale of the house. Anyway, the Training Center is where pilots go every six to twelve months, and whenever they upgrade or change airplanes. Basically, every time a pilot walks through the door there your career is on the line and your license is in jeopardy—a way of life that airline pilots adjust to.

Anytime things seemed a little overwhelming at "Stress U," I would pull out that bid award and read: *"Richard Wellington Jr., you have been awarded CAPT,*

737, BOS, effective date 1 January 1997." This was what it was all about; what I had worked for my whole life. After fourteen years of military flying and ten years of airline flying, I was finally there.

Marie was excited and *busy*, as things were happening fast. The boys were also excited but a little sad about leaving their friends in San Antonio. They were Texans through and through. At ages eight and five, moving to New England was something very different than what they were used to. It was an adventure though, and because we had family there, both boys took comfort in knowing that they had a lot of cousins waiting for them up in Maine.

Marie and I decided that things were moving so quickly that we would just rent a place for the first year or two, probably an apartment. That would give us time to prepare for the purchase of our "dream home"—the home we planned to grow old in; the home that would represent our last move in life; the house we would live in forever. That was a comforting thought, too, since all I had known my entire adult life was moving every few years. This move, however, was going to finally provide the stability we were looking for.

I took a lot of heat from my family and friends about moving "up north." I have always been a huge fan of the south, and the south is where my friends and family live. I knew no one up north with the exception of the in-laws. The fact that I had moved so much in life, and had always figured out how to make myself happy anywhere overrode the anxiety about moving to the cold northeast. I was getting what I wanted—the Captain's seat. Eventually, the house and all the trappings would follow suit.

****

We found an apartment in downtown Portsmouth, New Hampshire, just across the Piscataqua River that separates Maine and New Hampshire. The apartment was nice, but small for a family of four. Most of our belongings were in storage close by so we could go get and exchange things as we needed them. We also had covered parking in a parking garage nearby that we leased. We had two brand new all-wheel drive vehicles for getting around in the snowy winters of New England.

Within just a couple of months after learning of my transfer and promotion (my "upgrade" in airline talk), we were all settled in. I never thought I would enjoy downtown living, but I did. Actually, I loved it. Looking back on it, those simple times of apartment living in a downtown area were some of the happiest days of my life. We walked to the boys' music lessons. We walked to get a slice a pizza. Life was pretty worry-free and fun. The raise in pay without a mortgage payment was also nice, and the rent in our apartment, even for New England, was very affordable. We weren't hurting for anything. As pilots loved to say in that era, "I was *living the dream!"*

Our plans were to wait a year or so to be financially ready to buy the *dream home.* We got involved with a church, with school for the boys, and with sports. Well, I should say involved with hockey, since we were quickly becoming a fanatical hockey family. Hockey was the only sport our boys played, and we found ourselves in cold hockey rinks day in and day out for many years to come. It was kind of unusual for a family to move from Texas and go so full tilt with hockey, but we did. The boys were actually quite good.

After a few months we decided that it couldn't hurt to start *looking* at houses, so we did. For some reason that I can't even recall, very shortly into this process we had a real estate agent. This proved to turn our *looking* into something else, since I don't think there is an agent on the planet that ever really takes you out to "just look." It quickly became an all-consuming task, which makes one lose the whole sense of "I thought we were just looking."

Next thing you know, we were making offers and were on a full-scale attack of finding a home. Did I mention that this was months before we said we were going to do this? How about even a year or so prior to really being ready? Did I also mention that living in New England, real estate-wise, was exponentially more expensive than living anywhere in Texas? Oh well, it didn't matter! I was a *major airline Captain* making a lot of money, with even more to come down the road.

In this area I never really had the ability to say no to anybody, including myself. But why should I? We were on the fast track for success. We weren't the kind of family that had ridiculously expensive taste; we just didn't have it in us to defer gratification. We had earned it, so if that's what we wanted, then that's what we would do. I had thought that way for years. No, I had thought that way my whole life.

Just prior to going on a work trip I found a house listed online that seemed to have the perfect workshop, or barn. In New England the larger homes seem to have "barns." These are not necessarily used anymore for cows and horses and such, but are either an extension to the house or a completely separate building for a variety of uses—an ultra-large workshop to a recreation room to office space for a home business, and so on. This particular place listed for sale seemed to have an unusually large barn, separate from the house, finished, and heated, which really interested me.

I asked Marie if she could get in touch with our agent to see this place while I was out of town. Well, Marie did what I asked and went to see the house that had the barn. It was a nice New England Colonial that was on about four acres, on a quiet cul-de-sac in Kittery, Maine. Marie thought long and hard after seeing this house. Although it was nice, it was not *her* dream home. She loved its setting and location, and it certainly "had potential," she said. But she had to think long and hard about it. Barring an absolute refusal on her part, she knew that once I saw the barn, we would buy it, period. She knew enough to know that this barn was pretty much any man's dream shop, especially a man who likes to restore cars.

The barn had three levels, a full basement, a hydraulic lift, hot and cold running water, an office area, bathroom, and a total of over 3,500 square feet. I had been restoring cars my whole life, and this hobby was certainly part of my plans for the future. Being of British descent I was a fan of

British automobiles. I had owned lots of them. Triumphs, MG's, Jaguars, and I even had hopes of owning a Bentley or a Rolls Royce in my retirement years. Marie certainly knew whom she was dealing with. I wasn't overly materialistic—this was just a wonderful hobby. And why shouldn't I have this kind of hobby? After all, I was an airline pilot. I had a lot of time off and I certainly made an above average salary.

Well, Marie decided to give me the green light for making an offer on the house, *if* we did some major remodeling and architectural changes to the house. Of course I agreed, as I was now in "la-la-land" over this house! I would do whatever she wanted to make this house her dream as much as the barn was mine.

Have I mentioned yet that we hadn't so much as taken a pencil to a piece of paper over the financial side of this? The one ingredient that was sure to make all this happen was that I made very good money; financing was not going to be a problem. When the money people, however, put their pencils and calculators to it, it became evident that we were on the very edge of affording it. We certainly qualified for the purchase, and that was good enough for me. Being on the edge didn't matter. To get our foot in the door was supreme. I was on a mission, and we were going to purchase the place in Kittery, Maine that had the dream barn.

Being on the edge financially in the beginning, although a little risky, was still somewhat a viable plan, if dealt with head-on in the future. (That's where things get a little murky, as you will soon see). We were well-established with a certain lifestyle, and that life must go on, right? Our finances were somewhat stable, but we were still quite leveraged—no, *over* leveraged.

In our defense, if my career continued on the path it was on, the cash flow would continue to increase. Every time there was a new contract between our pilots union and our airline there was an increase, and sometimes a very good increase. When I went from First Officer to Captain, there was a *very* good raise. Other increases could be expected as your seniority increased or if you moved to a larger aircraft, which also paid more. There were also longevity increases, but those stop around the fourteen-year mark.

As one of the major airlines, we tended to get what others got or lead the way with whatever the next contract was going to be. I will explain. If another major airline and its pilot group was up for contract renewal prior to us, and they got a good deal, then almost all the rest of the major

U.S. airlines would follow suit, when it was contract renewal time. It usually never happened without a fight with management, but it would eventually happen.

Well, we had been living in the *Captain's* home about four years or so, and life was about to get really good for us, financially speaking. The airlines were doing great. Pilots with three other major airlines that were ahead of us with their contracts had just received the best deal I had ever heard of in the airline industry. It was huge! *This was finally going to be it,* I thought. This was going to be in the realm of "hitting the home run." See, as a family we didn't keep elevating our lifestyle; we were just over leveraged with the lifestyle we had. We paid all our bills on time, but we needed to get rid of some of them. This was going to be the *relief,* the final adjustment that we needed.

****

Now, let's forget the money issues right now. My story has much more to it than money, and a large part of that was my job. I loved being an airline pilot. I don't believe there was a pilot alive that loved *everything* about being an airline pilot more than I did. People who knew me from way back, realizing that I had accomplished my dream, would ask, "Is it as good as you imagined?" I would always say that with the exception of contract negotiation time (hence, the fight with management), it was even better than I ever imagined. I truly loved it, and would have not switched places with anyone anywhere. I was not envious of other professions or the amount of money they made. This career was the best one in my eyes.

One reason I loved flying so much was that I had grown up in this environment. My father had been an airline pilot. In awe I watched him walk in and out of our house with his uniform on, carrying his suit case and flight bag. I listened to the stories about the cities he visited, the restaurants, the hotels, the amazing sites. I was the recipient of gifts that could only come from certain destinations. To me it was magical; it wasn't "work," as I heard him always say. As a pilot, even though my dad was gone when he went to work, when he was home (as in all day), he was not at work. And he was home as much as he was gone, or more. I, too, learned to appreciate that aspect of being an airline pilot, which complimented my role as a husband and a father. I may have been gone more than most dads (not home every night). However, there were times that I had weeks off, or three or four days off in a row, and not because it was a holiday weekend or vacation. That was the norm.

All the benefits I witnessed as a kid I was now experiencing as an adult, and carrying on the same traditions of lots of time spent with my wife and boys. It could not have been better. There was only one thing on this planet that I loved more than my airline career, and that was my family. One supported the other as my family was proud of me and encouraged me in my career. We enjoyed time together and made life fun! We knew we were blessed.

One day I was scheduled to go on a trip to the west coast, which included a long overnight (layover) in my favorite city in the world—San Diego. I traded my trip with another pilot, however, because I needed a little extra time at home to work around the yard. We had that ability to move our schedule around as long as someone else wanted to fly the trip. I wanted to do some extra *special* yard work because an old friend from the military was coming, and I wanted everything to be perfect for his visit.

There was a project I had been meaning to accomplish for some time. It was a beautiful September morning. I mean the weather was perfect! The air was clear and dry, not cold nor hot; it was just right for what I had planned. I went down to the local rental center the moment they opened to rent a brush mower. I was pretty excited about getting this work done. See, in the very center of our cul-de-sac there was a common area that I referred to as the "giant weed ball." It would take a brush mower to clear and some creativity sprucing up the rest of the area to really make it presentable. There were a couple of trees and large rocks, and if landscaped properly, it could look nice but still natural.

I was cutting through the "giant weed ball" with the brush mower when I saw one of my neighbors approaching rapidly. I'll never forget the look on her face as she appeared quite disturbed. I thought, *Oh no. Maybe I should have asked for permission to do this, and cleared it with all the neighbors.* Before she got to me, I shut down the mower and started in with, "Don't worry, it's going to look good. . ." when she interrupted me. "Rich, I'm not worried about that, do you know what's going on?"

After she told me, I immediately ran inside to see on television the horror of what was happening. Yes, that terrible day was September 11, now known as *9-1-1.* The phone began ringing; everybody I knew wanted to know whether or not I was flying. My father called and was quite relieved to find me at home. He stated that it was very hard to get through, and shortly thereafter the phone lines died. It was a day that rightfully can be compared to the attack on Pearl Harbor, and a day that has not only changed our country, but has forever changed our world. From that day forward, I would *never* view my profession of airline pilot the same.

****

Immediately following this terrible event, there was a period of turmoil and unrest all over our country, but especially in the airline industry. The skies were literally shut down. New government bureaucracies were formed, and new rules were made. Businesses, including airlines, were filing for bankruptcy. Employees were laid off and salaries were slashed. At first it appeared that I would be all right at my airline. As I mentioned earlier, we were already a contract *behind* some other carriers. Staying at our current level of pay would be somewhat similar to a pay cut. Even though a salary cut threw a wrench into my "life is going to get really good financially" philosophy . . . well, I suppose, that didn't matter. It was now about *survival*, and everything appeared that we as a company, and as a work force, would do just that.

I could talk for days about how terrible it was—from the security procedures that harassed crew members (without making travel any safer), to threats from some airlines to fire employees who profiled Middle Easterners. This perfect job that I had always wanted suddenly turned terrible. The next hit was the new contract that was shoved down our throats, which made massive work rule changes and slashed our salaries. Possibly worse than all of that was the loss of respect we once had as a profession. At least in my opinion, that respect was gone. I realized that I could no longer be happy here, period.

I have greatly condensed the details of how my job changed. There were several years of dealing with a miserable existence as a pilot of which I'm not even scratching the surface. Some pilots may not have seen it this way. For them, their career was tarnished but still okay, and I'm not on a crusade to change their minds. For me, however, it was over and done. These were desperate times, and I began to search my soul about what to do. I was on a quest to shift gears, do something else, and I did not know what that would be.

One thing that made it more difficult for me was the fact that I liked my job so much. Between the military and the airlines, I had enjoyed my occupation of aviator-pilot for more than twenty-five years. That fact, I believe, actually worked a little now to my disadvantage. I realize that many people hate their means of employment, but they must continue to do it, day in and day out, for the paycheck. I was in the same boat as far as the paycheck was concerned, but this was the first time ever that I really loathed my job. Someone might say, "Spoiled brat, welcome to my world!" And they would be correct. I had always been blessed with employment that was exactly what I wanted to do. I worked hard to get there, but nonetheless, it *was* what I wanted to do. I now seemed to live in a different world.

I don't think the traveling public would believe the pure stupidity that seemed to reign supreme in how some airlines were run after 9-11, during those times of change and high security. Employee morale was at an all-time low. Airline management turned one group of employees against another. No one, and I mean no one, got along. The pilot group was always a huge target because of our salaries. Of course, management never liked to talk about their salaries, which were downright ridiculous considering their poor performance. They desperately argued that they had to offer management personnel high salaries in order to retain the "talent." We never saw much talent.

If you are still skeptical about my opinion of their talents and abilities, let me tell you a story. This is just one small example out of many. One month I was flying several trips that are called "turns." Unlike trips that were two, three, or four days in length, "turns" were just out and back in the same day. That meant I had to commute several times from home to the airport that month, but occasionally this was a nice break from packing a suit case and going out of town. So, I had a month of turns from Boston to Cleveland and back. These turns meant we were not going to layover.

Most of the traveling public incorrectly describes what a "layover" is. I hear people say, "I had a two-hour layover in Kansas City." This drives me nuts! My response is (of course, I'm only *thinking* this), "No, you did not! A layover is when during a flight trip, airline crew members go to a hotel and spend the night; hence, "laying over." When you sit around a terminal for a few hours waiting to change planes on a connecting flight, that is connection time, sit around time, time to eat a cheeseburger, or whatever else you want to call it, but it is not a layover. That's what constitutes the "turns" I'm referring to. We fly to Cleveland, sit around a few hours, and fly back to Boston. We are *not* laying over. Again, sad to say, even airlines are now calling the time in-between flights a "layover," so it's not the traveling public's fault, I guess. It's a case of word evolution, or rather, the meaning of the word was changed by continual misuse.

OK, back to the story. One night, while boarding the last flight of the day to go back to Boston, we were in the cockpit getting things ready to go. The gate agent came to visit me. She was young, energetic, and really seemed to be trying to do a good job.

"Captain, we are going to have some late connections, only by a few minutes. Since it is the last flight of the day to Boston, I'd like to hold this flight for a few minutes, to accommodate everyone," she told me.

I said, "They bought a ticket to Boston, let's take them to Boston!" I agreed wholeheartedly. I reassured her that we would probably still make Boston on time, as we had a tailwind. I thought, *Finally, an agent that doesn't seem to hate pilots or passengers.*

Then, in came someone whom I will call "Junior Management Man." This was an individual who was at the lowest level of company management, but was "management" nonetheless. This person happened to be male, probably about age twenty-two, was wearing a coat and tie and a reflective vest, and was armed with a radio. In general, "Junior Management Men" didn't like pilots.

It was departure time, and he stated, "Captain, I'm shutting the door."

"Wait a minute," I said, and reiterated that we were waiting on connecting passengers as previously discussed with the female agent, who was also standing right there.

"No, we're not. We are having an *on-time* departure! It is company policy that until we leave the gate, the company is in charge of the jet, not the Captain."

I could tell that the nice young agent was embarrassed, but she could not override him. I thought, *How stupid.* I was furious as the manager shut the aircraft door, disconnected the jet bridge from the jet, and walked back into the terminal.

I could now see through the window that there was a crowd of people at the gate, who also seemed furious. You guessed it, our connecting passengers. I immediately called our ramp tower (our own company-run tower for the gate area and a higher level of company management). I thought they would see it my way, since my only desire was to accommodate these passengers. Surprisingly enough, the ramp tower person told me the aircraft was already "clocked out" on time, and that sometimes it makes sense to do this.

"It makes sense to leave passengers behind, who are actually here?" I asked.

He replied, "Yes, Captain, you are out. You have departed, period."

Is your blood boiling yet? Mine sure was. Imagine being in that crowd. They probably ran about a mile from one gate to make it to this gate. They saw the jet still there, only to be denied boarding.

Well, it got better. The tug driver hooked up to the aircraft called me on the interphone system, saying, "Captain, it's going to be a few more minutes before we are ready to go down here, because we have some bags to remove."

"Let me guess," I answered. "You have to remove the bags from the connecting passengers who were not allowed to board this flight?"

"Yes sir, that's it."

That little procedure took longer than the time it would have taken to reconnect the jet bridge and allow those passengers to board. So, they sent some angry passengers to a hotel, and we sat on the ramp for fifteen minutes as the bags were removed. Oh, and guess what? We made it to Boston on time just as I had predicted—we had a tailwind.

Don't think for a minute that the airline removed their bags for the convenience of the passengers, who found themselves spending the night in Cleveland. No, the airline is required by the federal government to remove their bags for security reasons, since they were not traveling on the flight. And it would be a miracle if all the *correct* bags were removed.

The next day I contacted a Chief Pilot, someone in management that I still greatly respected and trusted. I told him the story. He did a little snooping around in the computer, and said, "Rich, this will make you even madder." Evidently, Mr. Junior Management Man typed some remarks in the computer, as they do to help track boarding/departure delays. He annotated that he had to "force the issue to have the plane depart on time," in spite of the fact that the "Captain demanded certain bags to be removed." Totally false.

That same company used to really care about its passengers and its employees. That same company used to make me proud. This type of mismanagement was rampant. It did not matter how hard I wanted to do a good job or how much I wanted to keep a good attitude—that was what the airline pilot faced. My dream job was crumbling.

****

I now cleared approximately $4,000 a month *less* than I used to clear. I tried desperately to make up some of this difference by working extra flights as the contract allowed, but that was not an easy task. There were thousands of us trying to do the same thing. But even working almost all the time still didn't come close to my old paycheck. Remember I stated before that Marie and I were *over* leveraged financially? Well, now we really were. We began using lines of credit, selling belongings, anything, just to stay in our house.

For a long time I viewed our house as something it really wasn't. I saw it as solid security for Marie, Richie, and Jack. I wish I hadn't done that. As Marie says, "Would-a, could-a, should-a—didn't." If I had admitted financial defeat, we could have stopped the bleeding earlier, and probably not faced such difficult choices later. But I didn't. I kept hoping that it would all work out. I just felt that the house represented too much. It all seemed to be unraveling and I did not know what to do. First my job, and now our dream house might be going sour, too.

I refused to allow this financial crisis to prohibit any family-related activities, such as sports and music lessons. In this way I tried to insulate my family from the problems. I succeeded in that area, but failed miserably in another. For the first time in their lives my boys saw their dad utterly miserable. I may have done a good enough job juggling finances so life could go on somewhat like normal, but I did a horrible job hiding my feelings. I'm not one to hide my feelings anyway; what you see is what you get. I was saying "yes" to anything they wanted, but I was making them all miserable with my demeanor.

I despised the airline industry so badly that one day, in front of my sons, I said, "I wish I had never learned to fly. I hate airplanes." Both of them looked at me seriously, and said almost in unison, "Dad, it's not the airplane's fault." Some statements just stick and that one surely did. Later, that statement would not only encourage me but also comfort me.

Fortunately, since I was a young boy I have had a strong faith in my God. Nevertheless, I was not displaying much of that faith right now. You could almost say that in the faith department, I was a "fair-weather flyer." As long as things were good, it was easy for me to feel adamantly about the blessings that I enjoyed, and to believe that they came from God. However, I never much wanted my faith to be tested with such difficult times and trials. I guess this is where one determines if his faith is *genuine*. I've heard it said, "Faith after the fact is not faith."

There's an analogy that is often used comparing an earthly father and his son to the Heavenly Father and His children. Just as I would never wish bad things on my children, I would want to teach them how to handle such things. I also may even allow them to experience difficult, even *very* difficult circumstances in order for them to grow, mature, and develop into successful thriving adults. *Maybe this is what God wants for me*, I thought. Well, if so, I certainly wasn't very victorious with it yet.

I felt trapped and didn't know what to do. Some days were better than others, but for three years I was searching; searching for an escape. I thought long and hard how I could get out of this flying business altogether.

****

One day a little glimmer of hope came to me. It started with a recollection of the statement my boys had made:

"Dad, it's not the airplane's fault." Suddenly, I was on a mission. It came to me that I *can* enjoy aviation again, I can stick with it. Something else in the aviation world will surface if I put my heart and soul into finding it. I had no earthly idea how I would do this. I needed to make a good six-figure income to stay afloat, but I was on a mission nevertheless.

I incorporated into my thinking that I *can* do this. I was a very qualified pilot, and had at that time over 14,000 hours of flying time, numerous jet-type ratings, and I was helicopter-rated as well. I had over fourteen years of active military duty, and maybe that could be incorporated into this quest as well. I started on a new résumé, and started reading every type of aviation publication I could get my hands on about different facets of the aviation world. I had been so isolated in the airline world for so long, that I knew very little of what else was out there. I had become a hostage to my airline without ever really realizing it.

My game plan, albeit unsure at this point, had one major theme: *I would find other employment.* I was approaching fifty, and at fifty years old I could retire early from my airline. The retirement wasn't nearly as good as it was crafted to be at the usual retirement age of sixty. However, it was a "bird in the hand," so to speak. Some airline pilots had lost much of their retirement through bankruptcy courts. This "retirement" was not going to provide enough for us to actually retire, but it was a way for me to leave the airline industry, without throwing it all away. I still had to find employment, and finding it at a high enough salary was the difficult part. But my attitude was starting to change from bad to a little better; one with hope!

By this time I had flown for almost thirty years, over half of that time with the airlines. Needless to say, I had a lot of dreams about flying and being on trips. I'm talking about literal dreams while I slept. The dream I had quite regularly was what I will call a *frustration* dream. I dreamed that I was running late (something that was very much *not* my nature or habit). Or I dreamed that I couldn't find my suitcase or flight bag, or I couldn't find my hat or coat. Bizarre things, too—that I was walking through the airport with no pants on, or trying to fly the wrong airplane (one I wasn't trained on). The list goes on. I had a lot of frustration dreams about flying and being at work.

One of these recurring dreams would eventually have a huge impact on my life. Mind you, I had been out of the military (U.S. Army) for a long time. Yet, the whole time I was at the airlines, I continued to dream that I was back in the Army flying the Huey helicopter, which was the first aircraft that I flew in an active Army unit as a regular mission pilot. So, in this particular dream I was back in the Army flying the Huey, but I was constantly telling everyone, "I'm not in the Army, I'm an airline pilot." Everybody said "Sure," and treated me like some kind of nut. This dream was like a nightmare. Now, I don't want to compare this to the dreams combat veterans have recalling terrible wartime experiences. This was just an incredibly frustrating dream. I was always trying to prove my point, which I never did. This dream came with some regularity for about fifteen years, off and on. Let me add that it was always nightmarish, at a minimum very irritating and negative. Little did I know, but this dream would change everything.

I am not trying to *over* spiritualize or *under* spiritualize this experience. You be the judge. I'm just reporting my experience—a very *genuine* experience. This negative, troublesome dream of mine eventually just miraculously changed to something totally different.

In the new dream, I was back in the Army, retired from the airlines, and it was a *good* thing. As a matter of fact, it felt like a great thing! This was one of those dreams that was so incredibly satisfying you didn't want to wake up. I did wake up though, and I thought that maybe, just maybe, I found a missing piece to the puzzle. This missing piece was a small but incredibly important part of the overall path I would take. My family had no idea what they would hear from me at breakfast the next morning.

After breakfast our family had a "morning meeting." In the mornings we gathered together as a family and shared our plans and concerns about the day ahead. We read a few verses from the Bible each day and prayed for one another. Although I was in the middle of some of the more trying times of my life, these morning meetings were a source of strength and comfort.

What I shared with my family that particular morning (my idea from the dream the night before, of retiring and re-joining the Army) was received well. However, I don't think they thought what I was proposing would actually happen. I believe my wife and kids viewed this as just one of "Dad's ideas," and this one was a little crazier than usual. It was a noble idea, but a little crazy.

I was forty-nine years old at the time and had been out of the military for over eighteen years. My sons had heard my Army stories, but my military days were all before their time. I had my doubts about my plan, but there was something about that dream that made me feel as though I was heading in a direction that I was destined for.

****

I got on the phone and started calling numbers associated with Reserve Officers in the United States Army Reserves. After explaining my situation several times to several different people (who also probably thought I was a little crazy), I had a packet emailed to me entitled: "Application for Direct Appointment to Warrant Officer, United States Army Reserves." The bulk of the Army's pilots, or "aviators" as they call them, are warrant officers. I had been a warrant officer, then a commissioned officer, when I was on active duty. I discovered that I was too old to go back in as a commissioned officer at my previously held commissioned rank, but I was *not* too old to go back in as a warrant officer at my previously held warrant officer grade/rank. That was fine with me, something I had already assumed. And I was off and running to try and get back into the United States Army Reserves as a Warrant Officer Aviator!

My plan was that after I got into what is called the Individual Ready Reserves (IRR), I could then find a

Reserve or National Guard unit to join, and thus complete my Army career (completing twenty years of service). As you would imagine, filling out all the forms related to the application and completing all the requirements of this direct appointment request/packet was no small task. I was consumed with this and worked tirelessly on it for well over a month.

By now my family knew that I meant business with this, and they supported me one hundred percent. If accomplished, this would be one form of employment that could replace a portion of my airline income—not much of it, but it was a start. Additionally, if I completed my Army career, I could look forward to a military pension at age sixty. I thought if I could retire from the airlines after I turn fifty, be back in the Army Reserves, and find some other civilian employment, then maybe I could make this all add up. I would no longer be held hostage by an industry I now despised.

There was something else that helped motivate me that was no small source of strength and encouragement. The attack on this country that took place on September 11, 2001, was what destroyed the industry I once loved. Our country was deeply entrenched in the War on Terror, and if I could get back in to serve, I would be honored to be a part of that fight. I had always preached to my family that it was the military that opened up a lot of doors in my life, and to that fact I would be forever grateful. This was my opportunity to serve again, put my money where my mouth was, and set a tremendously good example to my boys.

This glimmer of light, this small possible piece to the puzzle, gave me some hope. My overall attitude and demeanor improved. I genuinely felt that my prayers were being answered.

Back to the paperwork involved with this task. Thank goodness I had kept good records of my prior military service. In places where records were supposedly stored within the Army Reserves . . . well, guess what? They either weren't kept well or they were lost. Fortunately for me, I had kept my Official U.S. Army microfiche. Without this I would have been dead in the water. This microfiche was old technology; small pieces of film that has tiny pictures of documents on it. Each sheet probably contained about forty to fifty documents. This microfiche had all of my important records on them, which I needed to print out.

The Army didn't use this technology any longer, as all records are now stored on computers. I needed to convert my microfiche to paper documents, and then they could be scanned into the Army's computer system. Luckily, I found a public library that had a microfiche reader and printer; and after a few days of work there, I had the documents I needed. I also put together quite a portfolio of letters of recommendation—from retired military officers, a chief pilot at my airline, and people I thought would enhance my request.

I am only summarizing the overall requirements of this application packet. Completing it seemed to be a career in itself. Approximately a month into this process, I was ready to send it in to be checked for completeness and eligibility. At that point, my packet would be transferred to the board to determine if Richard Wellington Jr. would be allowed the privilege of serving his country again. I found out that the initial review process would also take a few months to complete.

My acceptance was contingent upon passing an Army Flight physical and being awarded a security clearance. I thought that both of those requirements should pose no problems, because I continued to pass an FAA flight physical every six months, and I once held a Top Secret security clearance. Again though, these were all lengthy steps in the process. One of the steps, in particular, gave me a run for my money: the physical.

The deadline for the physical was a few months away, which was a good thing, since this was not going to be an easy task. First, there were no Army bases near where I lived; and second, when you try to schedule something when you're not in the Army, it is hard to get someone on the phone who has a clue what you're talking about, even with the "letter of instruction/authorization." But this difficulty and delay would actually turn out to be a blessing.

One day I just happened to think about a concern. I had an issue with my left ear because a doctor had placed a tube in it at one time due to a sinus infection. The tube/perforation was to be temporary and removed later. The hole was supposed to close and the tissue was supposed to grow back together. Well, you guessed it—it did not grow back. I had even had surgery to repair the perforation, but after a week or two post-surgery, the hole opened up again. I was infuriated with the initial "doctor" (for lack of a better term), but it did not keep me from passing the FAA/civilian, First Class flight physical, so life as a pilot went on normally.

When I was about to schedule the Army flight physical, I thought, *Hmm, I wonder if this perforation thing is okay with the Army?* I decided that I better check that out first before scheduling the Army medical examination. After reviewing the Army regulations online, and even conferring with a military flight surgeon friend, I discovered that I would *not* be allowed back in the Army as an aviator without first having the eardrum successfully repaired.

I scheduled an immediate appointment with the same ear, nose, and throat doctor (ENT) who performed my first attempted repair surgery. Knowing the urgency of my request, he recommended one of the best ENTs in the business. (He also knew deep down how wronged I was by the other doctor who messed up my initial tube insertion procedure. But getting them to throw stones at each other is a near to impossible task.) Oh well, my faith teaches me to forgive and not hold grudges. It was my prayer to just get this eardrum repaired soon!

All through this frustrating process I just kept thinking about that new dream I had had. It *genuinely* seemed to point me in this direction. I wondered that if this was truly destined for me, if God wanted me to do this, then why was it so difficult? I had to *genuinely* believe that all would be fine in the end, but I must admit my faith was being tested.

Within days I had an appointment with the new ENT, the highly acclaimed specialist. He was an incredibly nice person. He had performed hundreds if not thousands of these procedures and was quite confident that he could repair my eardrum permanently. He too all but signed an affidavit that the first ENT botched the job. He jokingly asked if the first guy had used a quarter-inch drill bit and garden hose to accomplish the venting of the eardrum procedure. I liked this guy from the very beginning. He was also a private pilot and owned his own airplane. There was definitely a mutual respect between us pilots. Not only that, but he had begun his medical career as an Army doctor. He repeatedly thanked me for my efforts to return to military service, especially during a time of war. Surgery was scheduled within days of my original appointment. If that was not a divinely orchestrated event, I don't know what is!

So almost five months from the beginning of this albatross of an application to return to military duty, I found myself waking from another dream—in the recovery room. The required tympanoplasty surgery was complete, and my new ENT friend came in to see me. He felt that the surgery was a success, but he wanted to see me in two weeks to confirm. At a follow-up appointment, he gave me the same results.

To this day my eardrum is normal and healthy, *without* a hole in it. I will always feel a debt of gratitude to that doctor, and I have totally forgiven the first doctor for botching my ear. I have a normal ear again, and that's all that matters. Not only did the specialist come to my rescue; in my mind, he is also a patriot and a fellow flyer.

I was now approaching the sixth month of this process. Can you spell *frustration*? I finally had my Army flight physical scheduled. I traveled to a base in upstate New York, spent a couple of days there, and left with mostly reassuring news. I say "mostly reassuring" because my physical still had to pass the review of the U.S. Army Aero-medical branch at the Army Aviation Headquarters. Of course, I had to disclose the ear issue and the surgery, which was completely acceptable by Army regulations as long as it proved to be successful.

After waiting another two weeks, my Army flight physical was passed! I was deemed medically fit to return to service as an Army Aviator. I also received news that my security clearance was a go. My packet now passed the completeness and eligibility muster. My fate was now in the hands of a handful of Army Officers trained and assigned to make these types of personnel assessment decisions. There was nothing more I could do but wait.

****

I, Richard Wellington Jr., do solemnly swear . . . Yes, that's right. I finally took my oath of office and was sworn into the United States Army Reserves, Chief Warrant Officer 3, as an Army Aviator. From dream to reality, just months away from turning fifty years old, I found myself back in the uniform of my country. (I had gone to U.S. Army Flight School thirty years earlier, and would later serve with aviators who were not even born when I first received my wings.) A month after taking the oath I found a Reserve unit to join relatively close to home. I began drilling with them one weekend a month, and participating on other days with additional flight training periods.

There were a lot of challenges coming up ahead for us, including a one-year deployment to a combat zone. But the day I took my oath was a very proud moment. It was surreal, and I felt that I was *genuinely being directed* to accomplish what started out as an enjoyable, seemingly whimsical dream.

Oh, and remember the other dream that I had experienced over and over for fifteen years? The one that was nightmarish about being back in the Army? To this day, I've never had that dream again.

****

At least one piece of the puzzle was complete now that I was back in the Army Reserves. This accomplishment certainly hit the peak of the roller coaster ride I was on, but now it was back to reality. The airline industry was still a depressing place to work, and I wanted out as badly as ever. But my wife Marie kept telling me, "One day at a time, Rich, one day at a time."

I still planned to retire from the airlines at age fifty, and my birthday was just a month away. But I also needed to seek replacement civilian employment. That could prove to be an especially tough challenge as well. At least now I knew that I would have the opportunity to finish my military career and end up with a military pension at age sixty. This was especially helpful because what I would receive from the airline retiring at fifty was much less than retiring at sixty. Of course, leaving then with *something* could be better than staying ten more years and leaving with *nothing*—who knew where this industry was headed? Besides that, I questioned whether or not I had it in me to stay any longer than I absolutely had to in an industry that was miserable at any level.

During all of this time spent pursuing my new dream, nothing changed on the home front with the "juggling" of finances. It was depressing. I was trying everything I knew to stay afloat, which meant to stay in our house with the huge mortgage and also attempt to find new employment. It all just didn't add up; something somewhere had to give.

There were some civilian pilot jobs I could seek, but I did not know how I was going to afford them. Even after the huge airline pay cut, I still made a salary much higher than starting salaries just about anywhere else in the pilot world. Then it hit me. What if I took my retirement in a lump sum? I could take a hefty slice off the top, pay down our debt, and pay the penalties and taxes for early withdrawal. We could adjust our lives to live on less for the next couple of years, with the hope that in the near future my income would be back up to a level that would make everything doable. Marie and I discussed it and agreed. I knew of several civilian flying jobs, and if I could get one of those, this was a viable plan.

Well, another peak of the roller-coaster ride was about to be crested. I had a good friend from my old Army days that had a great corporate flying job. He had been there awhile and they were looking for a pilot. After looking into it, I found out that the starting salary was good; the benefits were great, including a very good retirement plan. I had enough time to actually create a third retirement! It appeared, from the company's predicted future growth, that I would be hired as a First Officer and then move over to the left seat within a year or so as a Captain. The Captain's seat paid what I needed to make my plan work. As long as it happened within the next couple of years, all would be okay. Remember, we planned to restructure the finances in our life to not require the higher salary for a couple of years.

In an unbelievable turn of fate, we discovered that this job would not require us to move. The company was located close enough to where we lived in Maine. The office was in Concord, New Hampshire, and the jet was located in Portsmouth, New Hampshire. It was also a very military-friendly company. They knew that I was in the Army Reserves and that there was a potential of being activated and deployed. The CEO was a retired military officer himself and did everything he could to support veterans and people still serving. In spite of the fact that they would need to temporarily fill my position if I was activated, I truly believe it was my story on how hard I fought to get back into the military reserves that landed me this job. Yes, you heard it right, I accepted their offer! I had just turned fifty and could retire from the airlines. I had a sizeable amount of money in the bank, a retiree medical plan, airline passes for life for Marie and I, and a plaque for the wall.

More than anything else, I knew I had a family that loved me. They all supported me through this long process from start to finish. I so much wanted to show my gratitude to them, and I did that by working hard so we could stay in what I thought was our symbol of security—our house.

We started a new life so to speak, though all the things relative to home life—church, music, sports—they all stayed the same. Although pricey, our younger son even toured Europe one summer, playing the cello in a string ensemble. Life went on status quo, which was exactly what I was shooting for. The airlines could be a *good* memory; key word here—a memory.

****

Although we did not know it at the time, there was an economic storm brewing up ahead that would take two or three years to fully surface. Our plan was working (with one exception—the house). What didn't go according to our plans was that the economy would take a nosedive.

This fact delayed my upgrade to the Captain seat in the corporate flight department. That consequently delayed the raise in pay needed to continue to pay for the house, without draining our nest egg that was created by eighteen years of hard work at the airlines.

I tried to delay the inevitable, juggling our funds again, and always trying to shield everyone from the real issue. Until . . . one day Marie figured it all out completely. She stated, "We *will* sell the house." There was no fighting over this, not this time, and I knew that she was right.

It was such a shame that we hadn't come to that decision years earlier, because there was some freedom associated with it. Remember, it was never Marie's "dream home," although she had worked tirelessly improving it. She would have been happy to sell it a long time ago; something I really didn't know. The boys, however, didn't like the idea at all. They *did* see their symbol of security going away, and our oldest son Richie did not beat around the bush telling us how he felt. I understood where he was coming from and he didn't mean it maliciously. He was just hurt seeing his childhood home going away.

Like it or not, it was the right thing to do, and something we *needed* to do. This was going to be no small undertaking however, as the housing market was in the worst shape it had been in my life time. We also could not afford to sell it for a bargain basement price. We owed too much on it and desperately needed to make something from selling it. To add an extra scoop of pressure, I was informed that I was to deploy to the "sand box" (Afghanistan or Iraq) with my reserve unit. We had about ten months to sell the house.

I could sense bitterness in our family, and most if not all of it was aimed at me. They were right. It was all my fault. It did not matter how well-intentioned all my years of juggling were or how hard I worked. I had failed them. I had always been an achiever, a confident go-getter. For the first time in my life, I felt like an utter failure.

At this point in my life all I really wanted to hold on to was Marie, Richie, and Jack. Thankfully, we all had a strong faith in our God, who does not disappointment. Other people will let you down and fail you, but God never will. It was this belief in God's faithfulness that kept us together as a family. It also got us through yet another trial.

Fortunately, we lived in a very nice area, and there were people with money who would pay the right price for the right house in the right location. We had all of that going for us, with two exceptions. Our kitchen and master bathroom were *very* dated. We felt we would not get what we needed or wanted for the house without redoing them. Remodeling them both was still a gamble, with the housing market in the shape it was in, but we decided that we must do what we must do.

So, let me outline our next several months of fun. We were going to completely gut our kitchen and master bath. We were going to spend lots of money hiring someone to help us design and remodel them both, in the midst of already not having enough cash flow to stay afloat without juggling. All four of us would be required to do a lot of backbreaking work.

Marie handled the bulk of it. I still had to go out of town on trips with my civilian job. I also had two periods of active duty training ahead with my reserve unit (one period was two weeks long, one was three weeks). All drill weekends were mandatory, and there were additional flight training periods required, all in preparation for our deployment. The deployment was to be a year long. I did not want Marie to have to deal with this alone while I was gone. Richie was in the midst of applying for college and would begin college about the same time that I would deploy. Once I was deployed, Richie would be away at college, and that would leave Marie and Jack to deal with all this. We had to sell this house.

****

Fast-forward six months. A month prior to my deployment, Marie and I found ourselves on the way to a closing. We sold the house! I have skipped over the agonizing six months of enduring the kitchen and bath remodeling, the staging of our home by our real estate agent, and showing it for more than two months. What's important is that we did it. Our faith in God to look over our best interests is what really did it. We put in a lot of effort, but this feat was nothing short of miraculous, considering the current housing market and economy. We didn't make a fortune on the house, but we made some money. More important, we are not statistics in the worst housing market in history of my life time. We never missed a payment, and we avoided any form of financial ruin for being overextended with this house. This was confirmation in our hearts and minds that it wasn't meant for us to fail. However, it was now time to totally reevaluate our long-term perspective on what is important and what is not.

I had a deployment coming up soon, and we all were focused on that. Richie was accepted to college and soon would find himself living again in his home state—the great state of Texas. We lived with relatives, because that would be best for Marie and Jack once I was gone for a year. We paid rent; we weren't freeloading. We very much appreciated our family's kindness and open arms that welcomed us. The hospitality and support they offered was no small measure of love.

I fought the urge not to feel like a total failure. I didn't fight that too well sometimes. In many ways our symbol of American "success" was gone. I was in my fifties now, did not own a home, and we drove two older vehicles. There was pretty much nothing remaining that was proof of "living the American dream." I had sold cars that I had restored, tools, and loads of other belongings that I had acquired my whole life. Marie sold furniture and many treasures of her own as well. Much of this was hard, very hard, and probably even more so for the boys. I could have easily slipped into the doom and gloom of the whole "starting over" game. But once again, our faith in God and the cherishing of what was really important would see us through this.

Whatever belongings we had left we kept in storage. Keepsakes, permanent records, and things we either could not or would not sell—mostly things of value to us alone. All these changes and losses turned us toward God, which was a very good thing. For me, there were even tougher challenges up ahead. So we turned our attention to the wisdom, blessings, and promises of the Bible. Some words of Jesus came to mind.

"Do not worry about your life. . . Is not life more than food and the body more than clothing? . . . Therefore do not worry, saying, 'What shall we eat?' or 'What shall we drink?' or 'What shall we wear?' . . . For your heavenly Father knows that you need all these things. But seek first the kingdom of God and His righteousness, and all these things shall be added to you" (Matthew 6:24-25, 31-33).

Don't worry? Wow, that was a new concept for me. I had worried for years. It was now time to trust totally in our Lord and Savior.

I think it is pretty obvious that I've never been much of a money guy. I'm not cheap, nor am I stingy; *that* is a positive. I also like to give sometimes when it would be best to save; *that* can be a negative. Now I had to find some middle ground. I had a great job and there was time to recover, and for this I was most thankful. It was, however, difficult to have to work so hard at a time in your life when things were supposed to be more at ease. Maybe I had too many years of ease early on, and it was time to pay the price for them. We had to live within our means.

Many people might say that our government does not live within its means, and I would have to agree. Why the government feels that it is their responsibility to bail out anyone is beyond my understanding. No one bailed us out, and we weren't asking anybody to; we had to make some tough decisions. Not only is it not the government's responsibility to bail anyone out—it is wrong, because the government in itself does not have any money. The government uses *our money*! I wish people could understand the concept that it is not the government's money but theirs.

Marie and I grew through all this. We grew both in our relationship with our Lord and with each other. I have heard it stated that character is not built in luxury. I have to agree. Character is built out of hardship; even if you cause some of your own hardship. Character comes when you take the blame—the responsibility—for what you've brought on yourself, and stop making excuses for it all. There were outside forces at work that did not help our situation. Yet, I had no problem recognizing the error of my ways, a thing that is becoming a foreign concept in our society. In some circles it is seen as a weakness to admit you're wrong. I could not disagree with that philosophy more adamantly. There is great relief in admitting our errors. There is redemption and beauty in this process.

Perhaps there's no better example of this truth than the story Jesus told in the Bible of the prodigal son. The younger son took his father's inheritance early and squandered it. When he ran out of ideas and money, he eventually humbly admitted his mistake and came home. His father did not scold him or tell him, "I told you so." Rather, the father celebrated with joy that his son, who was lost, was now found.

Through all the ups and downs, our two sons saw our faith in action, and I believe that will forever influence their lives and make them secure. Even more secure than all the comforts and stability that I *thought* they needed through a house and an endless list of "things." Family and neighbors experienced firsthand that our Christian faith and our family were the things we cherished the most.

What would take place over the next several years for Marie and me would be the most wonderful, enlightening years of our lives, even though very difficult. Yes, there would be a house again, but this time not beyond our means. Yes, I was still fortunate to have jobs that I enjoyed.

I would work hard and so would Marie. But clinging to each other and to our God would allow us to overcome seemingly insurmountable odds.

Now I'm really living the dream.

My Dad

It was an exciting day in the summer of 1970. I was at the Los Angeles International Airport, boarding a huge Boeing 747, on my way to the World's Fair in Osaka, Japan. What made it even better was that I was with my favorite person in the entire world, my dad. I couldn't be happier. It seemed that life was perfect when my dad and I were together.

This tradition of going on vacations—just the two of us—started several years ago, following a family vacation to Disneyland. It had been my dream to go to Disneyland, and for years my father encouraged me to save coins in a can labeled "Disneyland or Bust!" When our family got to Disneyland, my mother and sister complained that Dad and I "got up too early," "walked too fast," and "stayed up too late." My father made a command decision: "Next year, Richie and I will come back alone—just the two of us" And we did! We continued this new found freedom every summer, and now, here we were on a Pan Global Air Jumbo Jet about to depart for Tokyo! I couldn't help but be a little pleased that our original Disneyland trip went the way it did.

My attention turned to the stewardess who seemed to be approaching my father. I was only fourteen and a little shy about admitting that I now liked girls, but who could not be dazed by this attractive person? She was beautiful, and the pristine uniform just added to the beauty.

She asked, "Are you Captain Richard Wellington, from Louisiana Airlines?"

My dad answered, "Yes."

"Then what in the world are you doing sitting back here?"

She proceeded to escort us both to first class in this enormous, stately flying machine. As an airline Captain's son I was used to first class, but I never took it for granted. It was always appreciated, *never* expected. My dad worked for Louisiana Airlines, an up-and-coming national carrier. People seemed to love the company, employees and passengers alike. I think my dad loved it more than anyone, and his sense of loyalty to them was unwavering. That being said, this was Pan Global Airlines, the world's *premier carrier*. How they knew who we were at the time baffled me. Later, I learned that there was camaraderie among airline employees, especially flight crews, even when they worked for different companies. This perfect day and all its experiences seemed to have no limits. I was so thankful for being who I am. I am the son of Captain Richard Wellington.

****

Wow, these first class seats are comfortable. I find myself shutting my eyes and thinking about *Disney II*—my name for the vacation that started the whole "Dad and me" tradition. My mind wanders. *I wonder if there will ever be a Disney III? It's been an exciting day so far and I can't keep my eyes open. I'll just rest a little bit. It's a long flight; I'll just shut my eyes . . . .*

"WELCOME TO DISNEYLAND" the sign reads. It is early, and even though the park isn't open yet, the parking lot is crowded. Why are there so many cars in the parking lot this early? We drive forever, it seems, to find the next available place to park. The guides tell us exactly where to park our car, but I don't want to be in a line and wait forever to get in! *Disneyland, Day One, just Dad and me. Wow! This will be fun.* Rows and rows of cars, but finally we park the rental car. "Hurry up, Dad, let's go catch the tram!" I yell. We dash out of the car and catch a tram almost instantly. Our timing is perfect. *That's the way we operate*, I think, *and nobody is here to complain.*

Dad already has our tickets so we don't need to stand in the massive line to buy tickets We march right up to the park entrance at the precise moment it opens. Dad and I start walking—*fast.* "To the Matterhorn!" he yells. I cry, "Yes!" We begin jogging, laughing all the way. We both know what we're laughing about. It is freedom—*freedom to be us!* We are on the first run of the Matterhorn ride that day, and proceed to ride it over and over. There are no crowds this early. *That's the way we do it,* I think.

****

Ding! "The Captain has turned on the fasten seat belt sign. Please return to your seats and fasten your seat belts. Thank you for your cooperation."

I woke up to the smell of food. Dad had put my tray table down and the stewardess left me a meal, a *first class* meal, I might add. The food in coach was good, but the food up here was great. Besides food, there were playing cards, a miniature plastic 747 toy jet, a little Pan Global lapel pin, which I immediately put on my coat, a few stickers, and some postcards with Pan Global jets on them. There was baked chicken, some rice, some green stuff I passed on, and banana pudding and cookies. This was the life!

Three hours into the flight, we weren't even close to being half-way there, but who cared? This was fun. After the meal, the stewardesses offered us different chocolate candies. I picked the chocolate covered cherries. Later, Dad said, "Let's go for a walk." We headed towards the front of first class to find something I had never seen in a jet before—a circular staircase. Wow! We took the stairs to a lounge, with fancy chairs, tasty little snacks, sandwiches, chips, and drinks. Next, we saw something I never would have believed if I hadn't seen it with my own eyes. There was a small piano there with a man playing it! I was in heaven. *This is the genuine deal,* I thought. *First class all the way.* We were being pampered in every little way. This was a world I never knew existed. Life was good for the Captain and his son.

Back in our seats I decided to do a little reading from my book on Hong Kong. After the World's Fair in Japan, we were going to Hong Kong. This flight was long enough to help you realize that this is one big world we live in, but it also made it seem a little smaller. It was now easier to grasp that all different types of people in all different types of places existed all at the same time. Reaching distant shores and fulfilling dreams seemed a little more attainable. That's the way my father has always made me feel. He would constantly tell me, "Rich, you can do anything you want to, as long as you want to bad enough." I didn't realize it at the time, but that statement would live with me, and prove itself time and time again, for the rest of my life.

It is a wonderful feeling to be so loved, and I knew that was why my dad did so much for me and encouraged me. He taught me so much about everything. He was my source of knowledge, not only because he knew so much, but primarily because I knew that there was nothing he would not do for me. Pure and simple—he loved me and I loved him. I wanted so much to be like him. Again, I realized how thankful I was for being who I am.

I am Captain Richard Wellington's son. Richard Wellington Jr—that's my name, too.

Like a Bad Dream

It is day 321 of deployment to a combat zone, with another 44 days remaining. Who's counting? I am. You know that old cliché, "It's like a bad dream"? Well, right now that cliché is all too real for me. I'm in the U.S. Army Reserves, and my unit was notified almost a year out that we would deploy to Iraq. There is such a multitude of negatives involved in this experience that I don't know where to start when trying to describe them. I guess there is no better place to start than at the beginning . . . .

****

The misery started at the point of notification of our deployment. The usual Army reserves training weekends each month became mandatory and much more serious. Sometimes, due to one's civilian occupation, a soldier may miss the drill weekend, and just make it up later. Now, however, everyone was strongly encouraged (*forced* would be a better word) to be at every single training event. The Army has countless mandatory classes that every soldier must attend, and they are one hundred percent serious that every soldier—regardless of rank, position, or job—attends every single class. Most of these classes are painfully boring, and many of them have absolutely nothing to do with what you actually do in the Army on a day-to-day basis. I could talk a lot about this, but in the big picture of deployment this aspect is certainly small potatoes. I only mention it to explain that the tough tone was set for our military reserve unit and its schedule.

Our unit spent almost twelve months in training. Along with the monthly drills, the year included an annual training period of active duty for a couple of weeks. In my case, our "annual training" occurred twice—once for two weeks and another time for almost three weeks. This was more misery training with classes and running through wet, cold woods (even though we would be in the desert once we deployed). One of the worst parts of all this was the *joy of experiencing* the leadership (sarcasm added), or rather, the lack thereof. We had meetings to discuss when we would select the appropriate time to have the next meeting, along with dissecting every little nit-noid detail, ad nauseam, even though nothing happened as planned, schemed, or discussed. About the only other thing that took place in these marathon meetings was the annihilation of the character of anyone who happened to miss the meeting.

After twelve months of ridiculously stupid training, we headed to our mob station, short for "mobilization" station. This is something only reservists, guardsmen, we "part-timers/weekend warriors" do. Active Army units don't need to do mob station training because they are essentially ready to deploy all the time. Fortunately, heading to the mob station started the clock for the year-long deployment. That was not always the case. The mob station is an active Army post in the U.S., which *could* be an enjoyable time, but not for a deploying reservist. We don't get to enjoy all the comforts of main post, but are stuck out in the middle of nowhere so we can start learning how to be miserable together 24/7.

We were at the mob station forty or fifty days, or longer. Guess what we did there? Mostly we went to classes, many of the same ones we'd already had. Don't worry though. We had plenty more of those outside hot/wet/cold/tired/dirty/hungry experiences, too. We were also discovering the "joys" of communal living, the lack of any real privacy, the bad food, and losing some of our basic freedoms. Up to this point, however, the feeling that this was like a bad dream really hadn't overwhelmed me yet. Believe it or not, I, Richard Wellington Jr., was still proud that I was deploying to war. We all were. We had said good-byes to our families, but since we were still in the States and not in a combat zone, the reality of being deployed just hadn't hit us yet.

With our mob station training over, I found myself boarding a chartered airliner heading to the theater of operations (our theater being the Middle East). The flight was actually pretty nice, and the chartered airline personnel were friendly, patriotic, and supportive. I found it hilarious that we had to put our bags through X-ray machines and were treated the same as regular travelers. The toothpaste in my carry-on bag had to be less than three ounces, and I couldn't have any knives on me. That made sense, I guess. But considering that I was carrying an M-4 fully automatic assault rifle and an M-9 pistol, I must say that I had a hard time connecting the dots on that one. Once on board, I found it humorous to see the sea of weapons on this wide body aircraft. "Excuse me, but I believe that's my M-16" is not something you hear on most flights.

The airport security people the government had hired were real jerks. No other way to describe them. Ironically, they were all probably former service members so you think they would remember where they came from, but they didn't. They treated us all, regardless of rank, like we were lining up for chow at boot camp. However, we were treated well by almost every other person or organization we encountered on that day of departure. The USO personnel, veterans, and church groups were all good to us. We even had a police escort as our buses traveled from the boonies of the mob site to the local airport. There were free books, snacks, speeches, and inspirational talks that kicked off the day. It was obvious that this country had been deploying soldiers regularly for some time now. They had it down to a science. It made you very proud to be a part of something that others only read about.

It didn't take long, though, to notice the less-than-desirable attributes of being around a few hundred soldiers. For one thing, the language was embarrassing. I've never understood why so many soldiers—male and female alike—feel as though every sentence has to be vulgar. Most nouns, verbs, and adjectives used were a derivative of one particular word (yes, the worst one). Soldiers also quickly put to rest any fear that they may possess some class or social graces. It seemed that "passing gas" was to be expected in a large crowd of soon-to-be warriors; that would prove to get very old, very quickly. Remember, we were reservists and most of us had civilian jobs—many of which could never be retained with this kind of blatant, crude behavior. Oh well, hopefully the enemy would find them equally offensive. Like it or not, I was part of this unit for the remainder of this deployment.

****

We made several stops in Europe, and after thirty-six hours of flying (I'm *not* exaggerating), we were in Kuwait. We were shuttled to a staging area on some buses. They made us get off the buses, and then wait to get back on them. We were given one last opportunity to lose or misplace some of our gear, as we unloaded it off one truck to put on another. Everyone was tired and cranky, and we were repeatedly yelled at by various morons. This all didn't make any sense to me, but it's what we did. As soldiers, we realized that it was just another level of inconvenience and discomfort that helped complete the whole experience.

It was nighttime; it was dark, hot, and windy. The air was "crunchy," and we couldn't get away from the talcum powder-like dirt and sand that was in the air. There was a row of port-a-potties that could probably accommodate the crowds at most NFL stadiums. Not sure if they had been emptied in a while because the air reeked with the smell of human waste. *Get used to it, Richard,* I thought, as I knew there would be plenty more stuff to come. Three hours and twenty-two minutes later (again, I am not exaggerating), we finally got back on the buses. I heard that the bus ride to Camp Port-a-Potty (my new nickname for it taken from all the stories I've heard about its facilities) will be two hours. No problem. I just traveled from one side of the planet to the other, what's a little bus ride? Well, have you ever been on a bus where there is a rear end in every seat, and every rear end is carrying about a thirty-pound, overstuffed backpack and at least one weapon? I have now, and that bus ride started to test my limits.

The driver must have been a little warm because the air conditioning on the bus was set to about forty degrees below zero. It was freezing! I was crammed into my seat with my face in my backpack (which was in our laps per the directive by another insensitive, uncaring moron). I was trying to get into some position to sleep, stay warm, or do something to endure the ride without losing my mind. I quickly realized that just shy of an out-of-body experience that was going to be tough. I prayed that someone near the front of the bus would ask to *please* turn the air conditioner down or off. I think I quietly started chanting to myself, "Turn down the a/c, turn down the a/c," and eventually, someone in earshot of the driver asked him to please turn it down. Fortunately, the driver understood English and, even more fortunately, the driver complied. The sound of the fan at afterburner speeds was shut down. To hear it all go silent was most definitely an answer to prayer. I almost got emotional at that point.

Finally, something good happened, I thought.

As I was about to doze off, in spite of my seatmate's rifle stock pressing hard into my rib cage, something dreadful happened. The air conditioning went back to full tilt and the air was once again frigid. At this point, I wanted to surrender and we hadn't even met the enemy yet. Or maybe we had, and it was us!

We left the paved road and were on a rough dirt road that rivaled most motocross tracks. I've had back issues in the past. I wondered that if I had to be medically evacuated because of a back issue due to this bus ride, would I get a Purple Heart? Added to the back pain was the fact that I now needed to use the latrine badly. Once again, a moment of elation filled my whole being when we pulled up to a gate and stopped. I could see another sea of port-a-potties and I was not even going to mind the smell this time. Let me off this bus!

We actually stopped to get off the bus to clear our weapons. This is a procedure where you take your weapon to a fifty-five-gallon drum positioned in the ground. After ensuring there is no magazine in your weapon, you place the muzzle of your weapon in the drum, slide the bolt back to cock your weapon, and then fire it, proving your weapon to be unloaded. There was a line for all five buses to do that and it wasn't moving quickly enough for me. I still needed to go in the worst way! Finally, I cleared my weapon, and was running to the first port-a-potty I could find when I heard some jerk say, "No way, soldier. Get back on the bus!"

I almost cried when I told him I *had* to go!

He insisted, "No! But don't worry. The bus will stop just on the other side of the gate. There are more port-a-potties there, and it will only be a couple of minutes."

I should have said, "Shoot me—it's the only way you're stopping me!" But I didn't. I complied and got back on the bus. Twenty minutes later I was still crammed into my seat on that freezing, stinking bus. I was about to admit defeat and "water the flowers" right there in my seat, when a miracle no smaller than Moses parting the Red Sea happened. We stopped, and I found myself in line at a port-a-potty! It's the little things that bring joy. *Urinating without your bladder exploding would be one of those little things*, I thought.

We arrived at Camp Port-a-Potty, Kuwait, and went into a very large tent for another briefing. It was given by Private Snuffy (my affectionate nickname), who must have been chosen due to his complete inability to communicate in the English language. We had all been up now for almost 48 hours, and that tent started to look like an inviting place to sleep. Snuffy would have none of that though; he kept hollering for us to wake-up. What I got out of his briefing was a series of threats: "If you don't do this, . . ."; "If you don't wear this in this way, . . ." I wanted to stand up with a white flag of surrender, run, and hope that someone would shoot me in the back. At that point I was just plain ole delirious.

As strange as it might sound, everyone wanted the Kuwait experience to be as short as possible so we could get "in country," or get to Iraq. Though no one was shooting at us in Kuwait, there was a strong urge to be settled. Those who had been there before passed along that the living conditions were actually better when we got in country. In Kuwait, it was just a massive tent city with zero privacy. We all got to enjoy the nonstop swearing, snoring, flatulence, bad food, and those lovely port-a-potties. The initial stages of the "bad dream" were beginning.

I soon began to get a feel for the men I would be working for and with. Sometimes your immediate supervisor wasn't that bad, but the other guys you could never tell. You wanted to think that everyone in your unit was basically your friend, or at least on the same team, and that you actually knew the people you had trained with for the last several years. That was the strange part though. Some were my friends—the people I'd always known; others became entirely different human beings in this setting. They were the ones who constantly found fault with anyone who didn't think like they did. They were full of drama and not afraid one little bit to stab people in the back. Some of these guys loved to blame all the annoyances and personalities (like theirs) on the Army in general. I spent fourteen years on active duty in the Army and never came across such back-stabbing drama queens as these individuals.

There was another animal in our midst over there that was dangerous to morale. That animal could be called an "empire builder"—a person who tried to build their own little kingdom and get all the credit and all the rewards. Status quo was never good enough for the empire builders. They were not full-time active Army. No sir, they were reservists whom I thought I knew. Beware of the empire builder, close cousin to the drama queen.

I actually should not be saying this yet in the story, because at that point I was still naively thinking that we *could* trust each other. I couldn't imagine that there would be people intentionally trying to make you look bad. Goodness, didn't everyone realize that we were *all* making a tremendous sacrifice here? That's where logic might prevail, but that was not the thinking of the drama-queen crowd. Like the physical stresses, this relational stress started taking its toll on me. The bad dream was growing.

****

After a few weeks in Kuwait we moved "into country." In Iraq we were split up into four different bases; three were Forward Operating Bases (FOBs) with team leaders, and the fourth was Headquarters (HQ), where the command element was based. Everyone was pretty excited no matter where they were assigned; we were just happy to get settled. It would still be a few more weeks until we had all our belongings—additional duffle bags, footlockers, etc.—but finally we were making it "home." Well, sort of. Calling any of that a home started the "bad dream" feeling again. The good news was that the clock had started almost three months ago, which meant we only had nine months left until we were on our way back home. Nine months sounds easy enough, doesn't it? Well, not so fast. But it was still fortunate to have about three months of this misery behind us.

We ate up time assembling together at "home" preparing to depart, traveling to the mob station (staying there a month or so), traveling to theatre (almost a month there), and then traveling in country. We landed at the FOB (Forward Operating Base). Hadn't heard a shot fired at me yet, and I was just ready to learn my job and get about the business of completing this tour. The unit we were replacing was there for the next several weeks until they turned the mission over to us. This was first time we were actually doing our jobs. No more classes; this was the real thing.

I liked what I did as a reservist, but at this point in Iraq I still didn't *really* know what it was going to be like. By the time the other unit left, I did feel a sense of how I was going to handle it all. All the unknowns we'd been wondering about for a long time were starting to be pretty routine. Things settled in and for just a minute, you almost felt as if life was *somewhat* normal. Deploying halfway around the world away from family and friends, and being in harm's way is not fun. Those who tell you it is great are either lying or they have a real problem finding a meaningful life.

I was a pilot, or as the Army calls it, an *aviator*. I was assigned to an assault helicopter company, which primarily provided troops with the ride to the battle; hence, *assault helicopter,* or *air assault*. Things had slowed down and there wasn't a lot of combat, per se, going on right then. The coalition forces had the upper hand, at least for this period in time. We had largely transformed into what we called an "ash and trash company," meaning that we flew an assortment of missions just to keep things rolling. That was one of the reasons that we were split up in different locations, since we were to provide "lift support" to different locations in the country. Our missions included when personnel needed a ride from A to B, when equipment or supplies needed to be moved around, and the occasional air assault mission when fighting flared up somewhere in the region.

Understand one thing—it was not "all safe" over there, as the powers that were or as the media liked to portray at that time. By that time, I had been shot at, and that was never a good feeling. We got shot at while flying, and our base came under mortar, sniper, and rocket attack as well. I didn't mind the "ash and trash" missions because personnel and equipment need to get moved around. What I didn't understand was time we spent in what they called the "training mission." Now, let me get this straight. We trained in the States to come to combat, right? And now that we *were* here in combat, what else were we training for? To go back to the States?

My friend said we had to have the training missions for the slide presentations that the commander gives to the higher command. We have to look busy. Another friend in a medevac company (medical evacuation helicopter company) said they were not as busy as they were the last time they deployed, and they were going nuts with the training mission thing as well. They even organized a softball team and have "missions" to fly around and play ball! That's a great use of taxpayer's dollars, isn't it? Now, it was a very good thing that the medevac company was not flying much, because that meant that U.S. soldiers were getting wounded less. Not only was it good that less soldiers required immediate helicopter transport for medical care, but an added benefit from a reduced demand was that flight crews were exposed to less risk.

It was early in the morning, just prior to sunrise, on the first of March. I jumped out of bed and was putting on my boots when I heard the sound of a thud. I thought maybe it was some of the doors being shut in the building, possibly a muffled version of someone bumping a wall moving heavy furniture, or something much worse. The "something much worse" happened next, which made it clear it was another rocket attack. KA-BOOM!

That was close! I thought, as I quickly put on my Kevlar (combat helmet) and my flak jacket (body armor). Next, the siren sounded and I heard those dreaded words: "Incoming, incoming, incoming!" over the loud speakers throughout the camp.

It was a terrible feeling. You can train and prepare for it in every way possible, but until you experience it (heaven forbid you have to), you will never know that terrible feeling. That kind of experience never became normal or routine, nor should it. I was just as alarmed each time it happened as I was the first time I went through it. In some ways it became worse, because my ears became attuned to the sound of a thud. Many times it *was* the moving of furniture or a door shutting, but it still got my attention initially with the same sense of urgency and seriousness. I hope after I'm home that the wariness that goes along with the "thud" sound will go away.

There were some people who never seemed to get alarmed during attacks, or at least they didn't show it. Some of them balked at putting on their protective gear, trying to be "cool," or acting almost embarrassed to do so. This reaction would be one thing if it was based on confidence in a divine sort of protection, or something even logical about the possibilities or statistics. But I don't think it was. I viewed that type of behavior as irresponsible, cavalier, and careless, and definitely not cool. Being cool is *not* being foolish. At a minimum, if you are in charge of soldiers and you act like that, you are projecting the wrong image to those below you. This kind of behavior not only can prove damaging or deadly to you, but it can be a fatal example to others as well. Keeping one's cool means that in spite of what's going on, you maintain a level head in order to get on your gear and do what needs to be done, all the while considering the example that you are setting to younger, more inexperienced soldiers around you.

I found that most people didn't articulate well with either their actions or words. They constantly sent mixed symbols that caused confusion. Nowhere is good communication needed more than in life threatening situations. There were some soldiers over there that were honest with you, and who tried to do all the right things example-wise and safety-wise, but it was certainly not everyone.

Being attacked quickly cleared up any doubt as to whether or not that was a normal place to live. This was *anything* but normal or safe. Being attacked gave you the feeling of being violated, even after the dust settled and you realized that everyone was OK. This was not a feeling I would wish upon anyone, . . . with the exception of the people who launched those menacing acts of terror at us. *Normal* people in a *normal* world don't do this to each other. This was war though, and there is absolutely nothing normal about war. In a very short time my life as an activated reservist in a combat zone had changed everything.

****

After doing the mission day in and day out for several months, it became routine. Let me describe a typical day, week, and month. There wasn't much difference from one day to the next. Each day there were flights, as I mentioned earlier, for resupply, movement of personnel, an occasional air assault mission, or a quick reaction force mission (QRF). Sometimes two crews were on the QRF mission at the same time—which is a twenty-four-hour "stand-by to launch" mission. Almost without exception, if you weren't scheduled to fly a known mission, you were scheduled stand-by/QRF duty, with every fourth day off. Don't get too excited about hearing that we had a day "off." The concept of time off in the real world and being off here were two different animals. We were not flying on that day off, but we always had a boatload of other duties we had to perform.

A huge positive was that all twenty-five of us at the FOB had our own private rooms. This was exponentially better than sharing rooms or being in a big tent like we were in Kuwait, but there was not much to write home about with these private rooms either. In addition, we all had to share a big community latrine trailer that had toilets and sinks in it, as well as a shower trailer that had showers and sinks in it. I got up very early each morning to try and beat the morning rush to both of the trailers for the usual daily hygiene requirements. But that didn't mean I had privacy; it just meant *less* of a crowd. Other units (personnel) in the area shared those facilities, too. The next time you are all alone at home in your bathroom taking a shower, or taking care of other "business," take a moment to thank your lucky stars for the privacy that you are enjoying!

Day-in-day-out communal bathroom/ latrine living is terrible, and it takes more planning and effort than you might imagine. Let's go through a little of that planning. First, it was a good little walk to get to the latrine and shower trailers. You were always required to be in one of two complete uniforms—your normal ACUs (Army Combat Uniform) or your PTUs (Physical Training Uniform). You also had to have your weapon, possibly a flashlight (or headlamp), and whatever supplies you needed for the "hygiene experience." Somehow you had to have the ability to get undressed, dressed without your feet touching the horrible floor in the shower trailer, not get any of your clothes wet or dirty, endure the smell of the latrine trailer, without forgetting anything you need to do to accomplish this "mission," and/or forgetting anything you brought with you.

That was probably one of the hugest reminders every day that I was not home. Suffice it to say, it *was* all doable, but never as relaxing or enjoyable as taking a hot shower can be at home. Again, always be thankful for the privacy and lack of grotesque human beings living in your home.

Anyway, after completing all the steps necessary for routine daily hygiene, you were somewhat ready to start the day. Next up: time for breakfast. I always found myself in a long line that stretched just about halfway around the building. When it moved rather quickly, I was always thankful. I mentioned earlier that I had a friend in a medevac unit; well, they never even got to go to the chow hall. Due to the nature of being on-call all the time, they had to pick up their meals in Styrofoam® containers and boxes from the chow hall, and bring it back to their operations area. They had to divide up the duty for that job, and whoever was off-duty got to do that three times a day on their "off" day, including cleaning up the mess associated with the meals.

There was one thing we all learned to do over there: be thankful for your horrible life because somebody else always had it worse. With that in mind, a buddy of mine and I described the food that way. He would say, "It's *not* horrible." We had a sliding scale that ranged from "horrible" (the worst) to "*not* horrible" to "*not* bad"—this last one was close to "almost good," which was not even on the scale. Almost all of life over there could be described using that scale. The thing with the food was that, albeit, it was not horrible, it *was* pretty much the same every day, or identical for each day of the week. For example, every Monday was the exact same menu as every other Monday, "til

Kingdom comes, Amen." The variance determined by the day of the week was only for the main course; all the other stuff was exactly the same, every day, every meal.

There was also what could be referred to as the "poultry standard." I can unequivocally guarantee you, sworn to oath in a court of law, that there was some form of chicken for every meal, probably several forms—for variety of course. We joked that when the flags were flown at half-mast over there, it was for the *chicken genocide* that took place on a daily basis. If we stay in this war much longer, for sure there will be a worldwide shortage of chickens. I like chicken, or I *used* to like chicken. But when I got home, I didn't plan on lifting another piece of chicken to my face.

So the positive of this situation was, using an old cliché, that I ate to live; I didn't live to eat. That accommodated my losing about twenty-five pounds, which was a good thing. That was five more pounds than I really needed to lose, but I was sure that I would gain a little of it back after I got home. It is amazing how you can get use to smaller and smaller amounts of food. That didn't work for everybody over there though. Some people gained weight, lots of it. With three meals a day and every day, they were eating more and more and more. Even though the Army has weight standards there *are* a lot of fat soldiers. Pitiful to me, it was all a lack of self-control. It seemed that there were two types over there—those who lost weight and those who gained weight.

So, to summarize the eating situation, as you may have guessed, it was *not horrible*. From the chow hall we went to operations. We had a morning meeting and then usually either we went to pre-flight our aircraft for an actual mission, or we would pre-flight, and then run up the aircraft to sit stand-by/QRF, to fly if needed. And that was a typical day.

****

Believe it or not, dealing with all the *wonderful* living conditions (sarcasm added) was not a big part of the "bad dream" that was setting in. I have discussed the trials and tribulations associated with preparing to deploy and to settling in there. I have discussed the food, the latrines, and even the threat of being shot at. But I really haven't talked about the worst aspect of being in active service. There is no nice way of saying it—the worst part was the *people* with whom you worked every day.

Don't get me wrong. Some guys were my close friends, and without them the bad dream would really have been a nightmare, 24/7. But my close friends were just a few of the folks I had to interact with. I'm sure some people found faults in me and didn't want to see me every day either; so trust me, this was not a one-sided coin. Let me add something else though. I've been in other units that had a superb mix of people who were professional and enjoyable to work with. I did not, however, get the opportunity to deploy with any other units in my fourteen years of active duty. I know that no unit or group of people is perfect, but that mix was pretty unbelievable. In order for me to explain, I am going to try and describe a few of the people who made belonging to this particular organization the worst aspect of being there; the folks who give new meaning to the words "like a bad dream."

Let's start with Captain (CPT) Bob O. LaPointe, one of our pilots (*very* mediocre in the aviating department) and the Executive Officer (second in Command to the Commander). I also referred to him as the "Political Officer," as I believed that's how he sort of viewed himself . . . much like the officer the former Soviet Union had in each unit to keep them in line with the Party. He was a short Napoleon sort. What he lacked in stature, he lacked even more in personality, genuineness, and integrity. He wasn't an iota over five-foot-six inches, but he called himself five-foot-nine inches—perfect proof that he tried to overcompensate for his size. I'm not a tall person and don't care. I'm happy with how tall or not I am and what I am. What you see is what you get; no agenda period. CPT Bob, however, was nothing but a walking agenda, and it was all about him! Remember what I said about "empire builders"? Well, he was the best at it.

When you first met him, you thought he was a nice guy. You thought that because he latched on to you, educating you on just about everything. That was when you were new to the unit. Well, he had been there for over twenty-five years, so just about everyone was always "new" to him, and they would *stay* new to the unit in his eyes. In his eyes it was literally *his* unit and everything in or out had to meet with his approval. He loved to hear himself talk, and anytime he was given the opportunity to address the entire unit, he took it. He methodically waxed eloquent about anything and everything relative to how much he cared about our well-being as soldiers, solidifying the Commander's idea that this CPT was a wonderful leader and human being—when in actuality nothing could be further from the truth. He had sacrificed a lot for this unit; he had let his family self-destruct a couple of times over his loyalty to this unit. He had ex-wives and kids that hated him, and I'm sure they could talk for hours about their years of being manipulated.

CPT Bob liked to boast of his position in the Army Reserves, which was part-time. He loathed his civilian employment as a used car salesman. Guess that was where he learned his gift of gab, so to speak. There was one creature that he didn't like and was insanely jealous of—the *professional pilot*. He so wanted that full-time professional pilot identity. His license plate even had "Pilot-something or other" on it, and he tried desperately to build his flight time. A better way of saying it would be that he "padded" his log book, or that his pen "flew" for him sometimes. Let me explain. If two helicopters from our unit took off at the same time from point A to point B, and it takes the other helicopter (not Bob's) an honest 1.0 hour to fly the route; Bob's flight time somehow magically or mysteriously would be more like 1.5 hours. So what flight time he had managed to acquire had a multiplying factor built in.

As I mentioned, CPT Bob did his best to keep you thinking that you were new to the unit forever, as you would never be on par with him. If you "joined his team" and lived by his every word, he eventually gave you some sort of seal of approval. However, if he realized that you saw through him, you would become his arch enemy. Initially he seemed actually interested in you, drawing you in with that salesman-like demeanor. But nothing could be further from the truth. He was the biggest control freak I have ever met. He liked to send you down paths of destruction so he could come to your rescue, to ridicule you directly or indirectly behind your back and to get the glory he sought from the Commander for being such a caring, "in the know," critical-to-the-operation person. That was one of the things CPT Bob did very well—pull the wool over the Commander's eyes, and most everyone above him in rank. There was virtually nothing he would *not* do to please those above him, and basically nothing he *would* do to actually help those below him. All that mattered to CPT Bob O. LaPointe was that he would get more awards than you during the welcome home ceremony.

There was some justice, however. For some reason he never got promoted past Captain and so he never actually commanded the unit. Somebody somewhere in the chain of command saw through CPT Bob, and for that I am thankful. They also saw that he was willing to devote his entire being to this part-time employment in the United States Army Reserves, so his cost of labor was pretty cheap. It might have been a pretty good "bang for the buck" in that regard, but if they only knew the turmoil that he caused they might have reconsidered. He loved to be a "name-dropper" but appeared to have no real friends. I actually felt sorry for him. As mad as he made me at times, I couldn't help pitying him.

Next, let's meet one of the younger pilots in the unit. He is Chief Warrant Officer 2 (CW2) Clark Roads, an energetic, bright young man who was an attorney in the civilian world . . . well, sort of. Clark went through law school but hadn't passed the bar exam. He took the exam three times and from what I understand, he received a lower score each time he took it. I truly felt for him in that regard, as he went into pretty heavy debt going to law school, couldn't seem to get his credentials to practice law, and other than the deployment had no full-time job. That added to his frustration. "Am I a helicopter pilot (in Reserves part-time) or am I a lawyer?" he probably asked himself. Simply put, Clark seemed pretty miserable with life.

He had an identity crisis. He certainly was not a professional pilot, and was not even close to having the experience/flight time to be employed in the civilian world as such. And he wasn't really an attorney either. He was supposed to spend his time studying for the bar exam during deployment, but he found just about any excuse possible not to accomplish that. Unfortunately, this lack of self-satisfaction in life led Clark in the direction of stirring up the pot, so to speak, always bad-mouthing and being negative. There were other guys who created controversy for the sake of controversy. Many of them looked to an old-timer like CPT Bob as their example, and tried to emulate that "empire building" method in all they did.

Lots of people can identify with this relational and political strife no matter what their occupation is or wherever they live. One huge difference in deployment is that there is no getting away from these people. There's no meeting of the minds to make things better, because they specialize in turmoil; they don't want peace. I can't comprehend it, because there is nothing I despise more in life than turmoil.

****

So, I'm still counting down the days—44 exactly—til this deployment is over. In the meantime, how do I deal with the "bad dream" I'm living in? How do I handle all the difficult people? First, I try my best to "kill them with kindness." Next, I avoid them when possible. And in the end, I have learned simply to persevere and endure. That doesn't mean I do everything right. Tempers flare and harsh things are said. But I realize that losing my temper only facilitates their plans to create strife, which makes me try to avoid that at all costs.

I remind myself how thankful I am that I experience none of this craziness in my civilian profession. I am a professional pilot and have been for over thirty-five years. I work with other professionals who learned a long time ago that that kind of strife and turmoil has no place in the cockpit. Not to mention that a professional pilot would not be employed long using the types of tactics I came across in my unit during deployment.

Let me mention another thing that helped me deal with the tough stuff—my faith in God. Yea, I know, I don't sound like I have much faith, but it's there. No better place to look for help on this subject than in the Bible, where Jesus said, "Love your enemies, bless those who curse you, do good to those who hate you, and pray for those who spitefully use you and persecute you, that you may be sons of your Father in heaven; for He makes His sun rise on the evil and on the good, and sends rain on the just and on the unjust. For if you love those who love you, what reward have you?" (Matthew 5:44-46).

Of course, that's easier said done. But if we practice it, no matter how difficult the situation, it will bring relief. I tried hard to wish the best for Bob, Clark, and all the people associated with this unit. I tried to see the good side of them all. I knew that I was not supposed to be resentful, spiteful, or hateful. I also realized that I have flaws and have to look to improve myself. I must constantly look for ways to treat those around me with kindness. People who build their little "empires" would never think of relating to others like this, but thank the Lord, I can choose a different way to be. I made it a practice to pray for all the individuals who tried very hard to make my life miserable in that environment.

The Bible also tells us to do our jobs as if we were doing it for God himself, to honor Him by doing our best. "And whatever you do in word or deed, do all in the name of the Lord Jesus, giving thanks to God the Father through Him" (Colossians 3:17). Again, this is very hard, but it does bring humility and reward.

My time in Iraq has not been fun by any stretch of the imagination. Did you notice how most of the "like a bad dream" experiences I have related didn't really focus on the dangers of combat? Even with those dangers, with the right mix of people who were secure with their lot in life, it could have been a whole bunch more enjoyable. I must say that I am not even remotely trying to put this in the same category of the infantry soldier who faces severe danger, blood, and guts on a daily basis. His "bad dream" is exponentially worse than mine. My bad dream is one of repetition, separation from my family, the substandard living conditions, some danger associated with those conditions, and the immature and grossly under qualified, selfishly motivated leaders who constantly created strife.

Again, I look to Scripture to help me endure and cope, "We also glory in tribulations, knowing that tribulation produces perseverance; and perseverance, character; and character, hope"

(Romans 5:3-4). *Tribulation.* That's what this bad dream is all about. But the good news is that it can produce perseverance, character, and hope in me. It's not easy at times, but I am growing in the process of it all, and am still growing. I know in my heart that I volunteered to do this for all the right reasons, fully committed to the Reserves organization and its goals. The hardest part to swallow is the resentment, the jealousy, the lack of any patriotism of many in leadership positions, and the lack of respect for each other that I have encountered. That all adds up to making the bad dream of service one giant disappointment.

If I am a better man because of these experiences, then I thank God for all the trials and tribulations this ordeal has dealt me. As I search for the genuine remedy to conquer difficulties in life, the one constant theme is that God is so much greater than all my problems. I have learned that when I focus on His power, rather than on my weakness, in due time I will receive strength not of my own, but directly from the Almighty.

Family: The Story of Us

You've heard people say, "Think happy thoughts." Well, the thoughts that make me happiest are of my family: Marie, Richie, and Jack. I like my extended family, too; but this story is about my family of four. Marie and I like to call it "The Story of Us," and that's exactly what I want to share with you. If you don't believe that there is a Greater Power behind the scenes who is sovereign over your life, maybe this story will help challenge that thinking.

When I was a brand new commercial airline pilot-in-training, we had to submit a "dream sheet" of places we would like to be based after the training was complete. We called it a dream sheet because that's pretty much all it was—you would be based wherever the airline needed you.

Everything in the airline industry relative to its employees was done according to seniority. Being "new hires," seniority was something our training pilot group had very little of. I was talking to my father one day over the phone about my dream sheet preferences. I told him I wanted to be based in San Antonio, Texas, at the headquarters of the airline. The only problem was that it was a very senior base. Most of the new hires were being based in New York City, which was a very junior base. While talking to my father on the phone, he said, "If you *have* to go up north, you may want to try Boston." Being a southerner, I hardly knew the difference between Boston and New York, so it made no difference to me. Also, I was so excited about being an airline pilot after all those years of working toward it, that it really did not matter to me where I ended up.

The day came that we were handed our dream sheets with three spaces for our first, second, and third choices. There were nine total crew bases at the company, some much smaller/larger and junior/senior to one another. My class was the most junior new pilot class at the company, so we knew we didn't have much of a chance with our choices. My first choice was SAT (San Antonio), second was ORD (Chicago), and third was LGA (New York–LaGuardia). As I handed in the form, my father's suggestion went through my mind, . . . *If you have to go up north, you may want to try Boston.* I quickly asked for the form back, struck out LGA and wrote in BOS (Boston) for choice number three. It was totally unlike me to strike through something and write in something else, because I am somewhat of a neat freak, especially when it comes to printing and filling out forms. However, time was of the essence as they wanted our class to move on to other things and I certainly did not want to be the one holding them back. Did it really matter? No, probably not.

Much as we suspected, about two weeks prior to graduating from training my whole class of ten new hires was assigned to LGA, LaGuardia– New York. I knew that someday when I was senior enough that I could get San Antonio as a base; for now, this was just fine. Another week went by and we were all talking about how we would cope with living in or commuting to the Big Apple, when I got a phone call to my hotel room. It was a call from one of the administrative folks that did the crew base assignments. He relayed to me that it was very unusual for an opening to come available to such a small and senior base, but one just did. He saw that I had put Boston on my dream sheet, and asked, "Would you rather go to BOS instead of LGA?" He continued, "It doesn't matter to me. I need you in either place. Purely your choice." It really didn't matter to me either, as I didn't know one city from the other. But if my dad recommended Boston above New York, well, . . . I told him that I would take Boston!

That was the start of the adventure I sometimes refer to as "Jethro Goes to Boston." See, I'm as much a southerner through and through as any human can be. If you've ever been to Boston, you know that there is virtually nothing about Boston that resembles any aspect of the south—from weather, to mannerisms, speech, the pace in which people live, cost of living, etc. But soon I found myself in my truck on the way to Bean Town.

I rolled into a motel for the first night and was shocked by the price, which was quite high to me. It was right next to a shopping center and I soon began to get my bearings in the area. It was an older area, not that nice to me, but it would be the part of town that I became oriented to. It was not that far from the Boston Logan airport. They gave us time to settle in, but I planned to go the next day to the airline's Flight Operations, even though I officially did not have to report for almost two weeks. I wanted to go to Operations to check out the rooms for rent posted on the bulletin boards there. I wasn't planning on renting a room for long, because I thought I would just rent a small house somewhere. This was one of the reasons for the self-imposed title of "Jethro goes to Boston." I was totally ignorant of the cost of living, and renting a small house there was not going to be even close to affordable on a brand new airline pilot's salary.

A couple of days later I found myself renting a room in a lady's basement for more money than I ever paid for rent anywhere. It was a good thing I had saved some money in the Army as I knew that this transition from military life to civilian life would initially be costly. However, I had no idea it would be *this* costly. It would all be worth it, I thought, because someday I would be making the big bucks. The neighborhood that I lived in was somewhat close to the area I had first pulled into. So whenever I needed to go somewhere, I would make my way from where I rented the room to the shopping center as the start point. That was the day well before GPS's and cell phones, and one had to rely on maps, directions, and trial and error. I will add one caveat: Boston and its surrounding area is possibly *the* worst area to drive around in, especially when you don't know where you are going. The roads are paved forms of horse trails that were made about a million years ago. They aren't in square blocks, there are tons of one-way streets, and the drivers are the most aggressive humans I had ever come across, with little or no knowledge of the rules of the road. What do I mean by rules of the road? Rules that are observed all over this country, at least everywhere I've been, and there was none of that here! It would later lead me to coin the phrase when referring to Bean Town: "It's cold and expensive, but at least the people are rude and the traffic is horrible." I know that sounds insulting and for that I apologize. If you live in and love Boston, that's wonderful. To each his own, and I hope you enjoy it. I only mention my tough adjustment to all this because it still plays into the story.

The first Sunday I was in town I wanted to find a church to attend. There was a specific type of Bible-believing church that I wanted to find. I found one listed in the Yellow Pages that was close to the shopping center I knew, so I went to both the Sunday school, which was held in the main sanctuary for adults, and the main worship service. It was good, and the teaching was in line with what I was used to. The next Sunday came and I wanted to try another church that I felt would be a little more nontraditional—a little more "Spirit-filled" and lively was what I was looking for. After mapping out the way and even calling the church for directions, I started out very early that Sunday morning to find this new place to worship. I cannot describe how lost I got.

You know how when you are going down an expressway and you feel as though you've passed your exit, you usually just go down one more, exit, and turn around? Most parts of the known world may be this way, but not Boston! When you exit to turn around, you now find yourself on a new highway going who knows where. I was starting to doubt if I would be going to church anywhere that Sunday. I did not even know how to find my way back to the area that I was somewhat familiar with. Oh, that's right, *just stop and ask for directions* (sarcasm added). Remember "Jethro goes to

Boston"? Well, Jethro could not communicate very well with the locals. They use jargon for roads that only they know, such as "central artery" (pronounced "awt-uh-reeee"). Again, sorry. . . I'm not trying to be insulting. I have a *very* pronounced southern accent, so I realized that I was as much a part of the problem as Bostonians are. You can make fun of me all day and I won't get offended. But the point is that I may as well have been in the middle of Italy! We were not communicating, and there were no signs for the "Central Artery," you just have to somehow know what highway that is.

I stopped for gas and thought that I just might not make it to church that day. I saw a bumper sticker on the car next to me that had the name of a high school near the area where the "shopping center" was—the shopping center that was the new "center of my universe." I politely asked the folks if they could point me in that direction. After explaining where I was from (they heard my accent and just had to ask, *as always*), they were quite nice to me. They did chuckle a little every time I talked, but they sincerely wanted to communicate. They were surprised that I wanted to head that way, as I was nowhere near that area. They explained to me that they were heading over to their grandmother's house, info that really didn't seem pertinent to me, but I was grateful nonetheless for their help.

I drove for another thirty, forty minutes when, hallelujah, I saw the shopping center! I hurried and made it to the church I had gone to the week before. I felt like it was a miracle to be walking into this church! The pastor who taught the adult Sunday school class noticed me and sat down next to me to chat. I found out in our conversation that he was not from New England either, and I believe that played a little into his knowing how I felt. If there was ever a feeling of being "a fish out of water," this was it. He laughed about my abbreviated version of just being lost, asked about my work, where I lived, etc. He really seemed to care. I already felt more at home here and realized that maybe it wasn't meant for me to find that other church.

The church service was great. At the end of the service the pastor really surprised me; to say I was caught off guard would be a huge understatement. He asked me to come to the front of the church, so of course, I *had* to. He told the congregation: "We have a visitor today who is new in town. He's a brand new airline pilot, he doesn't talk like you people, and he's single . . . get the hint . . . someone take him home for lunch." Wow, was I red in the face. Almost immediately a couple walked up, introduced themselves as Leon and Sofia, and invited me to their house for lunch. I just couldn't say no, although socializing with complete strangers is quite out of character for me. Fortunately in all that happened, I believe there was a Higher Power in charge at the moment.

I followed closely behind the couple's car as to not get lost. In just a few minutes, we pulled into their driveway. Unknown to me, there was another part of this family in a car behind me, a part of this entourage. As I got out of my truck I almost knocked over this young lady with my truck door. Leon said, "Oh, by the way, that's my sister Marie." I thought, *Wow, I like Marie.* This uncomfortable situation was starting to have some real positive spin to it.

Leon and Sofia were about my age and had been married since college. Their children ranged from about two to seven. There was Anthony the oldest, then Mary, and Rose. The family lived with Sofia's mother, Lorina, and they had a teenage girl from Sofia's family living with them as well. Her name was Christy. Most importantly, Leon's sister Marie lived with them. I was immediately smitten with Marie. If there was ever a description of what I think beautiful is, she was it, period. Of course, there is much more to a relationship than physical attraction, but that part for me was completely out of the park!

Before lunch Leon and I were in the living room talking. I found out that he and Marie were from California. He had attended Massachusetts Institute of Technology, and while attending school he met Sophia. They married and moved in with Sofia's mother, Lorina. Lorina evidently had always opened her home up to those in need, and I'm sure there was some family situation explaining why Christy was there. I got the overall feeling that this was a very nice family. Leon and Sophia had the eventual goal of moving to Maine once Leon could find employment there. As to why Marie was with them, Leon explained that his sister just wanted to try something different from California.

In the middle of our conversation Marie came in the room and asked me, "How do you like your steak cooked?"

I paused for a moment thinking I didn't want to sound too picky, but knowing that I really don't like rare. Evidently Marie wanted a quicker response than I was giving.

She said with an irritated sounding tone, "You do like steak, don't you?"

I said, "Yes, very much so, just not bloody, any way except bloody."

Well, lunch was interesting and a little humorous. I sat down, the blessing was said, and out came all the food. The steak that was given to me was huge. When I saw it, I knew that I was in trouble and wondered if it was intentional to get back at my slow response. The steak was not only bloody, it was just a couple of degrees from a heartbeat, and I was convinced I could hear soft mooing sounds. I was going to have to fake it though, and that I did—*um-um-good.*

The fact-finding mission was going great. Christy was my source of information as she would not stop talking about Marie. She was evidently quite impressed with her. I found out all I needed to know in order to come up with a plan to ask Marie out on a date. Bingo! Marie was a hairdresser at a salon that I was going to find sometime during the week. I even found out indirectly what hours Marie was working so I could make my plan. Before lunch was over however, I gleaned some additional information that could facilitate a date happening even sooner. Evidently Marie was performing with a church group that very Sunday night at an outdoor service close by. Being somewhat in the area I was familiar with, I secretly planned on attending. After the service I would then find Marie, and ask her to go out for some pizza.

All went as planned to a point. I heard the group sing, found her after the service, reintroduced myself as the one who was at her house for lunch, and asked if she would like to go get some pizza. She answered no. That was pretty much it—no excuse, no waffling with her response, just no. Being somewhat embarrassed and extremely disappointed, I went back to my little one-room basement abode to contemplate the day. I still had plans for the haircut.

Soon I officially reported to my airline's Base Operations as a newly hired pilot. The custom was to report to the Chief Pilot the first time in uniform. I was very proud to do this as this was the first time I had ever officially put on the uniform. I felt as though I had waited a lifetime for this moment. The meeting was relatively short with a tour of the facility and a nice "welcome aboard" briefing. After the meeting I planned on stopping for that haircut. I thought this would be the perfect time to reacquaint myself with Marie and ask her out on a date.

Leaving the airport I went in search of the hair salon and once again I found myself lost, though not as badly as before since I was in the area of "my" shopping center. I did not want to call and ask; I just wanted to find the place. I thought I had remembered that Marie was working that day so I just wanted to arrive and get my haircut. That would bring up the perfect opportunity to get comfortable enough to ask her on a date. As I mentioned earlier, this was before cell phones and GPS receivers, so other than a map and directions (which I really did not specifically have), the only other way to find a place was to find a pay phone. So I drove through the parking lot of the shopping center where I think I see a pay phone. Then I notice something even better: a small sign with the name of the salon I was looking for. *Holy moley, this is it!* I thought. I was ecstatic. How did I not realize in my fact-finding mission that the salon was in *this* shopping center?!

I parked and walked in, and out of the corner of my eye (I was trying not to be too obvious) I see Marie at her station cutting someone's hair. I checked in with the receptionist and request Marie. In just a few minutes I was escorted to Marie's station. Somewhat surprised to see me, Marie said hello and was unpredictably quite nice. She seemed very confident and self-assured. I could tell that this was a very familiar environment for her—her "turf" so to speak. She was very easy to talk to, and genuinely seemed interested in talking. She asked all kinds of questions relating to flying, why I was in my uniform, and so on. I also noticed she had a Bible at her station. Not only did I like that, but it also gave us plenty more to talk about. Even though she made me feel very comfortable, I was still nervous. I got a wonderful haircut, had a great conversation, paid her, said good-bye, and that was it. I did not say one thing about going out to eat; I was just too nervous. Maybe I was scared that once again I would be rejected. Whatever the reason, the mission was incomplete. But I did have an enjoyable time.

The next Sunday I went to church again. I decided I wanted to attend there. I enjoyed the pastor's teaching, not to mention I wanted to see Marie again. I made a point to say hello to Marie before church started and just forced myself to blend that morning greeting into an invitation.

"Would you like to go out to eat after church?"

She looked a little surprised and a little caught off guard. Stumbling around a bit, she said "Well, my family usually has plans after church. I'll have to let you know after church."

It did seem to be a little glimmer of hope, but I didn't want to be too optimistic, as I certainly remembered the blunt "no" from the previous

Sunday night. Needless to say, I did not hear much of the morning sermon with this on my mind.

When the service was over, Marie came up to me smiling, and said, "Where are we going?"

Yes, yes, yes! I thought. Little did I know that my life and hers would change forever from that moment on.

We went to a steak place just down the road. The steak was good and so was the conversation. She asked me loads of questions. I had nothing to hide nor any problems answering each question in my usual quite detailed and confident manner. I would consider myself to be just about as transparent as a person can be, sometimes to a fault. I knew who I was and what I wanted to be. (I found out later that this was a quality that really impressed Marie.) The date went well and we had tentative plans to have another date in the future. We talked over the possibility of her showing me around some known landmarks in Boston. It was definitely a success. So we had our second date seeing Boston, and for a third date I rented a little airplane and took Marie flying. That was the first date that I was really comfortable with, being on *my turf.*

Fast-forward a year. Marie and I were married in that same church we both attended almost one year to the date of our meeting. How did all this happen? Remember that statement my Dad said? "If you have to go up north, you may want to try Boston." And the fact that I changed my base request at the last moment, listing Boston as one of my choices. Lots of moving parts here! There's only one viable explanation I can come up with in my own heart and mind, and that is a totally sovereign and loving God. When we listen to those small inner urgings, God directs our paths. Even when we don't listen, He can still guide us back on course.

This is what Marie and I call "the story of us." It didn't stop with just us though. Soon came our son Richie, and then son number two, Jack. God has had a plan for us all along, and I'm sure He has one for Richie and Jack, and their children to come someday.

Does it mean that all of life is easy with just one adventure after another following God's path? Not at all. There are good times and there are bad times. The key to getting through them all is remembering God's sovereignty. He has a plan so far above what we might think, hope, or dream. He is, however, interested in all *our* thoughts, hopes, and dreams. My advice would be to allow Him to open and shut doors as He chooses.

I'm very thankful for our story. I'm especially thankful for God's patience when I go off in the wrong direction at times, thinking I know best. God lets me learn from my mistakes and missteps, and all the while His love and concern for me never wanes. Even during periods of absolute disobedience my heavenly Father has never stopped loving me, never stopped wanting the best for me, never stopped trying to help orchestrate the "story of us."

I know this to be true. Our heavenly Father, even more than our earthly fathers, genuinely loves us and is totally sovereign in the affairs of the bigger picture of life.

Disappointment

It is Sunday afternoon and it is a beautiful day. We just came home from church ("home" for now is my brother-in-law's house), and we are greeted with a big welcoming banner saying "Wishing the Best to Rich and Richie!"—with pictures of a cap-and-gown graduate and a helicopter.

Our family and church friends are giving my son Richie and I a going-away party. We both are embarking on tremendously challenging adventures. I am deploying to the Middle East as a U.S. Army helicopter pilot in support of the War on Terror, and Richie is starting college. He's going to a school with a full-time ROTC program on a U.S. Army four-year scholarship. It is ironic that he leaves almost the same day that I deploy. Richie has his challenges coming, and deployment would be no cake walk for me either, at fifty-three years of age.

My wife, Marie, has been working tirelessly to make this party a great success. Fortunately, my brother-in-law's house and yard are both large as there is quite the crowd gathering. My mind rushes back and forth in an almost surreal way. *I'm about to say good-bye to everyone for an entire year,* I think. It sinks in, but not really. This is going to be a tough year for all of us—Richie, me, Marie, and Jack. For now though, it is time to enjoy the party.

"Hey, Rich, we wish you the best over there. We appreciate your service."

"Rich, my man, you are gonna make your unit look a lot better with your piloting skills."

Everyone keeps congratulating me and thanking me for my service. It really makes me feel good. If there is a common denominator among almost everyone here, it's their support for my going back into the military, and a sense of pride that our son is somewhat following in my footsteps. I have been a professional pilot in some capacity for almost thirty-five years, either in the military or as an airline pilot. I've actually been back in the Army Reserves now for three years part-time, and I fly the UH-60 Black Hawk helicopter. I hope they are right, and that I can make a good contribution.

I bring to the table a lot of flight experience; but most importantly in my mind, I have maturity, and a track record of making good decisions while flying all those years. Those are things that are difficult to teach. They come with time and experience; there's no other way of getting it. I feel good about what I'm doing. It will be difficult I'm sure, but I am glad to offer something back. I feel I owe a lot to the U.S. Army for giving me a shot at becoming an Army aviator.

My thoughts turn to Richie, about to embark on a tough challenge himself. He is attending a university that is a senior military academy. That means as a Cadet he will live the military lifestyle twenty-four hours a day, seven days a week. He will be in school for his next birthday (just a couple of weeks away), and I will be deployed.

I leave the party to retrieve Richie's graduation gift. I wrote him a long letter to go with his gift. Before I put it in the envelope, I read it over again.

Richie, Richard Jr., my buddy, pal, and son:
I thought I would give you your birthday card early, because who knows what your life or mine will be like on your special day in September. Whatever is going on though, I will be thinking of you.

I will never forget the day you were born. .
. . I will always remember it as one of the
happiest moments in my life. Mom and I have
been reflecting on the last twenty years these
last few days. Wow! You are going to be
twenty! It's a strange feeling to see your son
pack up and move on to a new life. As a
parent, you know it's coming, but I don't think
anything really prepares you for it.

Next, I want to encourage you with some
thoughts that keep running through my mind. I
am VERY PROUD of you. You have done an
excellent job following through on your goals
and objectives. You now find yourself at the
beginning of a monumental challenge. I know
in my heart that you are up for this challenge
no matter how daunting it may seem at times.
I'm going to pass along some advice and
wisdom my father always encouraged me with.
I know you've heard it before, but please don't
gloss over it because you have already heard it.
He used to say to me: *"Richie, you can do
anything you want to do, as long as you want
to bad enough."* Listen to these words like
never before and try to unlock the depth, the
motivating force that they provided me

through tough challenges. That is how Granddaddy lived as well. It may not be grammatically correct, and only applicable when in line with God's overall plan for your life, but its message is clear.

One of the most profound things that statement always said to me is that it is really up to me. I don't know how to describe wanting something bad enough, but that is what motivated me through Warrant Officer Candidate Flight School, later Officer Candidate School (OCS), and becoming an airline pilot. Becoming an airline pilot was a process that took over fourteen years, with many setbacks along the way. However, I never stopped "wanting it bad enough."

Now, I recommend adding something to that statement that will make it more than humanly powerful, but spiritually powerful. Add God's Word, the Bible, and prayer to your daily life. Scriptures such as, "I can do all things through Christ who strengthens me" (Philippians 4:13); "Seek first the kingdom of God and his righteousness" (Matthew 6:33); and my favorite, Psalm 91. Read that psalm often. Apply it to all your goals, use it to combat your fears, and you will find peace in the midst of the storm.

You will build your faith by reading and *believing* God's Word. I've always said I don't know how to explain believing, especially as it relates to faith. You simply must believe. "Faith is the substance of things *hoped* for, the evidence of things *not* seen" (Hebrews 11:1). God has brought you here for a purpose. He will see you through it, if you put your trust in Him and do not grow weary in well-doing.

I also want to encourage you with the fact that you are doing something very special. It is one thing to pursue a good education, but you are doing so much more than that. Being a member of the Corps of Cadets will soon become a huge part of your identity. Completing that education and getting commissioned in the United States Army is also so much more than just training for and taking on an occupation. I truly believe that becoming an officer in the United States military is the best foundation that a young man could have as he starts his adult life. Yours will be even more special because you earned it here in the Corps at this school that has such a tremendous reputation, and long standing tradition of creating superb leaders.

Your mom and I walked around campus the other day and I could picture you walking to class in your uniform. I also pictured Granddaddy here in his "pinks & greens," as he was here during the WWII era. He would be so incredibly proud of you. Don't ever be envious of the civilian students and their freedoms. Freedoms and privileges will return to you in due time, and you will cherish them even more when they do. What you learn along the way being denied freedoms and privileges is priceless, and unachievable by any other means. Pure civilian education is not even in the same league to one that includes a regimented military lifestyle. The high road is never the easiest road, and nothing in life that is really worth having comes easily. Make no mistake about it: this won't be easy; but you will make it. I believe you will not only make it, but you will also shine and flourish at this endeavor. It will take a little while and a lot of effort to get good at this new life. There will be a day in the not so distant future, though, that it will all make sense and feel normal. I have total confidence in you.

Lastly Richie, I love you. There's never been a moment, and never will be a moment, that I stop loving you. I will pray for you daily and cherish the thoughts of seeing you progress through this special time in your life. You make me very proud; give this endeavor your very best, walk humbly with the Lord as your Master, and never stop wanting this.

Love,

Dad

I slide the letter back in its envelope and put it in my Bible. I have to fight back the tears as I go outside and face the well-wishers at the party. So many people at the party pull me aside to let me know how proud they are of me, and to reassure me that they will be praying for my safe return. I see many people speaking directly to Richie as well, offering him the same assurances.

Marie has done an outstanding job putting this party together, I think. It is amazing how strong and organized she is, standing firm through all of this.

God has truly blessed me with the perfect wife; perfect for *me*, that is!

****

Several days later Marie, Richie, and I were in Texas making preparations to drop Richie off at a camp designed for new incoming freshman. Our younger son Jack stayed at home with his aunt and uncle. This camp was not yet the military side of things, but would still be truly educational and enjoyable for Richie. What was *not* going to be enjoyable for me was the fact that this would be the last time I saw him prior to my deployment.

Well, this was the day. We pulled up to a huge parking lot where other students were helping the new freshman unload their bags and send them in the right direction. I saw that this was going to be a quick process. I was getting nervous since I could get emotional in a split second. But I couldn't let that happen for Richie's sake. No one else there knew that this was my good-bye to my son prior to going off to war. I could tell that Richie was a little nervous, too.

We got out of the car, some kids grabbed his bags, Richie and I hugged and we told each other "I love you," and that was it. I spent almost twenty years of my life helping to raise this young man who has my name, and in a matter of seconds I said good-bye and it was over. It was a terrible, empty feeling, and I will never forget that moment. Two more moments like this were yet to come. I had the good-bye with Marie. She was staying there in Texas to take Richie to college after the camp. And I had to say good-bye to Jack at home. I dreaded them both.

On a side note, I had asked my Commander if I could stay in Texas and meet up with my unit there, since our mobilization station was also in Texas. He said no. It sure would have been nice if he had said yes. Then Jack would have come with us and we could have said our good-byes together as a family. It was disappointing, but he certainly had the right to say no. At that point I was still naïve and wanted to think the best of everyone with whom I was going to war; I just wanted to cooperate and get this done.

I had one day to be with Marie before I left. When the moment came to leave, I was clearly not ready for it. There was no way to be ready for that heart-wrenching event. She dropped me off at the small Texas airport; we hugged, kissed, cried, and said good-bye. It was starting to sink in that this was a *huge* sacrifice to make on all of our accounts. I gave her my letter written to Richie, to give to him before she told him good-bye—another terrible and hard moment for her as well. Later on the airplane, I wrote her the following letter, which I left beside her bed back at home.

To my dear wife Marie,

As I start this letter, I'm sitting on a Boeing 757, an aircraft I have over 3,000 hours in. I'm even sure that I have piloted this *very* aircraft, since I worked for this company for over eighteen years. But at this moment, that all seems like a million years ago. It almost feels as if it never happened. I just said good-bye to you; I already had to say good-bye to Richie; and in two more days I will be saying good-bye to Jack. This is the beginning of a journey only God could have predicted.

I just returned from the jet's restroom, or more accurately called the "lav." When I saw myself in the mirror, it was a reminder that I'm no longer a young man; however, God has granted me the ability and given me the assignment to go perform in a young man's world. At age fifty-three, almost fifty-four, I'm heading to war, literally. Not a figure of speech, but really a war, and the process and itinerary of it starts in just days. As a matter of fact, this trip is actually part of it. I don't say that to dramatize things or to worry you. I feel more prepared to do this now than at any age or era of my life. I am also grateful to be given the opportunity to do so. It's finally time in my life to be a participant in the saying "that freedom is not free." I think of the airline Captain I knew, who was brutally murdered by terrorists on that awful day that we now call 9-11. I think of an airline career that was altered forever by that dark day. That day was our generation's Pearl Harbor. This war on terror, no matter what they want to call it in today's liberal elite circles, is here to stay. It will only be altered by the efforts of the United States military and its allies; which is why I find myself in the middle of this surreal day.

Telling you good-bye is the hardest thing I've ever done in my life. You are my companion, my most trusted confidant, truly my very best friend. I don't know what hurts the most—whether it's the inability to be with you physically, or the helpless feeling of not being able to do all the things I usually do for you. I know you tell me not to worry, but that is very hard for me. There is nothing that provides me greater joy than providing for you, protecting you, and loving you. That will NEVER change. We've had our plate very full for a year or so, and the character that you have displayed through it all is nothing short of amazing. I'm not just saying that either, Marie. You are my inspiration to succeed, my motivation to be strong, and my desire to live. I love you more than life itself.

Lastly, sweetheart, I must take the time to thank you for being so supportive. You make this difficult situation so much more tolerable by your encouragement, your willingness to be tough and independent when needed, and your love. I started this off reflecting on patriotism and sacrifice, a willingness to serve. You should realize that you are serving, too. There's not one thing I do that is a shred more important than what you are doing. You are serving this country as much as I am. Without you being who you are, I could not do this. Our boys are sacrificing as well. I appreciate their willingness to support their dad. You have shaped them into fine young men and we are as a family very strong. We will make it through all of this and have better days ahead.

I must also remind myself that this season will pass. In due time we will be reunited and enjoy each other's presence again. I truly believe that the Lord has been preparing us for this for quite some time. I never imagined how I could ever really be thankful for trials or to count them as joy, as the Bible says, but I do.

Marie, thank you for being who you are. Thank you for being a great mother to Richie and Jack, and thank you for being my wife. As always, I love you more than I can describe.

Love,

Rich

Back home at my brother-in-law's house, I had a day and night to spend with Jack before I departed on the deployment the next morning. We attended the Army Reserves unit's official deployment ceremony, which was great. My church pastor brought a whole bus load of people to show support and tell me good-bye. There were hundreds of people there; many friends, relatives, politicians, and high-ranking officials to thank us, encourage us, and send us on our way. It really made you proud to be a part of this. Again, I was very naïve, patriotic, and so much wanting to serve that this sacrifice seemed worth it.

After the ceremony Jack and I went out to eat at one of our favorite steak restaurants. It was apparent that although we were thankful for and cherishing this time together, it was really hard to have fun. There were too many mind-boggling, heavy thoughts on both of our minds. Jack is a lot like me—sensitive and with a tendency to be emotional at times. I could tell that we were both already dreading tomorrow morning's early farewell. We had our steak dinner and went back to the house. I had a little more packing to do, then it was time to hit the hay. As I lay in bed, I read my Bible, prayed, and eventually went to sleep. There was a seriousness about the moment that was just almost overwhelming, but I knew I had to keep my composure through it all and do what I had to do.

The next morning I was up early and so was Jack. There was no attempt on his part to sleep in that morning. My brother-in-law was taking me to the airport, so my good-bye to Jack was to be right there in the house, and it was approaching rapidly. I had loaded my duffle bags in the car, and there I stood in my Army A2CU's (Army Aviator Combat Uniform), looking at Jack. We hugged, we cried, we talked, we said "I love you," over and over. To this day it is still hard for me to think about this. Not only was it an emotional moment for Jack and me, it was also the culmination of all the good-byes I had already experienced with Richie and Marie. I'm sure that it didn't help Jack that neither one of them were around at this moment. At seventeen years old he had to be incredibly strong and mature at this moment in his life. Before I walked out, I handed him the letter I had written to him. This is what I wrote:

> Jack, the Jack-ster, my little guy, my buddy, my pal,
> I'll start off with something very simple but something that is timeless: I love you, pal. I can't tell you what a joy it is to be your father. You make me proud with everything you do. You make being a parent easy and you always have. Don't think for a moment your cooperative spirit or kindness goes unnoticed. Your Mom and I are both very

appreciative of how enjoyable you are to be around every single day. That brings me to the sad part of this letter. I am going to miss you terribly. I look forward to being able to communicate via the phone and with email, as I will cherish being able to stay in touch with you. I must have plenty of doses of that "Jack-ster humor" . . . it will truly make my day! Please don't ever forget that! It's O.K. to be a little sad, just know that it is only temporary, and God will see us through this next year.

Now comes the responsibility stuff. Along with being proud of you comes a request as well. Now that Richie is away at college, you're now the big guy around the house! Mom needs you, and I know that you will be your usual cooperative, helpful self. You now face some tough challenges of your own. It is very important that you do some wise things now that will pay huge dividends later! When Mom and I come up with rules for things, it is not to make your life more difficult, but rather, just the opposite. We want to apply what we've learned from teaching and instructing Richie, and from our own life's experiences, and apply them to your life. These are all good things. Never before has the "cooperate and graduate" philosophy been more true and pertinent. I look forward to our family trip we have planned to celebrate your graduation from high school, and by then, you should be all squared away with your college plans. What you do NOW will help make all of YOUR DREAMS accomplishable.

That brings me to where I comment on YOUR DREAMS. Jack, your dreams are my dreams. There is nothing I want more in life for you than for you to be happy, fulfilled, with your dreams lined up with God's will for your life. I believe that God places dreams in His children's hearts. We've discussed many times about the things to be careful of and things to downright avoid. This letter is not about that. I have a lot of trust and respect for you. This letter is to assure you that I am behind *you and your dreams* one hundred percent. I don't ever want you to think that because Richie is going into a military lifestyle that I don't respect or honor yours. What you want to achieve will take just as much discipline and study as what Richie wants to achieve. In some cases, it will take more discipline, because it will be up to YOU to provide the discipline. Self-discipline can be very difficult, but with God's help I know you can do it.

· Lastly, Jack, I want you to know that this year will pass more quickly than you think. There will not be one moment of any day that I don't think of you. There is not anything in this world that I would not do for you. When I come home, we will settle in our own home again, you will be driving, and life will feel a lot more normal. I'm very appreciative of your willingness to make the necessary sacrifices, and know that this current situation is only temporary, . . . it will pass.

Jack, you are the son every father wants. Please don't ever forget how much I love you. Please be safe while I'm gone, help out your Mom (she's the GREATEST MOM on the planet!), and pray for old Dad while he's gone. I'll certainly be praying for you. I look forward to seeing you when I come home on mid-tour leave; I will be counting the days until then. I love you, Jack.

"Train up a child in the way he should go, and when he is old he will not depart from it" (Proverbs 22:6).

Love,

Dad

****

Many months have passed since those terrible moments of saying good-bye. As a matter of fact, my deployment year is close to being over. I elected to take my mid-tour leave around the nine-month mark, so when I come back here, I will only have a couple of months left. As I write this, I am only days away from getting on that freedom bird and heading home on leave. That will be the recharge I need to complete this terribly long, difficult year.

Remember the earlier story about my deployment experiences? It was all about the dirt, the filth, the communal living, and even the danger that made you feel as if you were smack dab in the middle of a *bad dream*. I discussed some of the personalities that made the experience worse. But they, too, could just be considered a side issue. Nothing could make all those inconveniences "convenient" however, with the right attitude and the right mix of people on a noble mission, those inconveniences would not be so noticeable. The story I want to share now is not about those details. Rather, it is the fact that this entire experience has all been *one huge disappointment*—on every level.

This is not a bad attitude talking; quite the contrary. I have worked very hard to keep my attitude in check. I will admit some days are easier than others. Nonetheless, dealing with this disappointment is something God has helped me with, and that is the positive part of this story. The Bible has a lot to say about our tough times and disappointments:

> Therefore, having been justified by faith, we have peace with God through our Lord Jesus Christ, through whom also we have access by faith into this grace in which we stand, and rejoice in the hope of the glory of God. And not only that, but we also glory in tribulations, knowing that tribulation produces perseverance; and perseverance, character; and character, hope. Now hope does not disappoint, because the love of God has been poured out in our hearts by the Holy Spirit who was given to us. (Romans 5:1-5)

The truth of this Scripture is powerful. It truly can help us endure life's difficulties, some of which are very complex and difficult, and that in our own strength may be impossible to deal with. I hope it will help you deal with disappointments after hearing the story of how God has been helping me.

Remember how everyone was so encouraging to me at the going away party, and so sure that my unit would benefit from all my aviation experience? And my noble thoughts that it was time to step up to the plate and bat against the War on Terror? Well, on all counts, I was wrong. I never would have imagined in a million years what materialized during this deployment.

After being in my Army reserve unit for almost four years I had developed a couple of very close friendships, and those remain constant. What I didn't know was how many other people would try to stab me in the back once they became empowered on this year-long active duty tour, nor that my previous experience in aviation would be totally shunned. I will go into more detail later, but simply put, I am not being utilized in any shape or form the way I should be utilized. I have been up for promotion almost from the first day of deployment, and that has been denied. I watch other men, who don't have a fraction of my aviation or Army experience, be promoted to positions they can hardly handle. It appears that CW3 Wellington will not ever be promoted to CW4 as long as this crowd has something to do with it. I see the blind leading the blind, and it is not pretty. But the worst part is the flying side of the equation.

The Army has what they call Pilots in Command (PC) and Pilots (PI). I am a PI (or as the rest of the world would say, "Co-pilot"). For some reason I am not a Pilot in Command, and I try my best to deal with that. There was a time that it made sense that I was not yet a PC, because I hadn't flown helicopters in many years. But I have been back in helicopters for almost five years now, and I had more helicopter total time than most of the younger PCs. My total flight time, air sense, cockpit decision making, and overall aviation knowledge was not even in the same league as the others. (I'm not trying to boast, it's just that I had been a professional pilot for almost thirty-five years; most of my PCs had not been alive that long.)

The most troubling part is that many of the younger PCs, plain and simple, do not want to listen to anyone else. It's interesting that the older, more experienced aviators have said that I should have been a PC a long time ago. I never had any difficulty flying with them. They saw the big picture and they were not threatened. They didn't treat me like the younger crowd treated me—like a child and as if I knew nothing. The more experienced aviators know how to communicate effectively, one of the most important skills needed to be a good pilot in a crew larger than one. All the flights I have had with the older aviators have been enjoyable, at least from a crew management perspective.

There is no enjoying the flight with the younger crowd though. They can't communicate effectively, and they are always posturing themselves to prove that they are in charge. They cannot take correction, let alone learn anything. It is absolutely a miserable cockpit environment. They have never learned one thing about what the airlines would call Crew Resource Management (CRC), originally called Cockpit Resource Management. No, they rule with an iron fist and that is it. The airlines recognized more than thirty-five years ago that running a cockpit that way is not the best or safest way to do things. I have been attending a CRC class about every six months for over twenty-five years. Yet, none of the young PCs in my unit want to hear anything from me other than "Yes, sir"... "Wow, you are so good"... and "Whatever you say, sir" . . . ad nauseam. They want to make simple things complex, which is the exact opposite of what a good pilot does. They are looking to impress you and live for praise of some sort. Sometimes I do "praise" them sarcastically, but they think I'm serious, and it is fun to watch them get all puffed up. (I have to have some joy while trapped in that machine with the absolute dichotomy of a professional.)

Not all the older ones become good pilots, either. Remember, most have not had good mentors. An experienced pilot can be a bad pilot, too. The older experienced crowd that has mastered his/her profession became that way because they have flown somewhere other than in this unit. I'm not a fan of the young officer going off to flight school in an Army Reserve unit or a National Guard unit and then staying in that unit forever. Don't get me wrong, that could work out well if you were fortunate enough to have the right foundation, or mix of professionals. But in the case of *this* reserve unit, it is certainly not the case. There is not a diverse enough level of aviator experience, but rather a hierarchical process of paying some dues, or joining the club. This process "eats its own" so to speak, and the best politicians survive—not the best pilots.

This being a copilot, evidently a *permanent* thing, has been a very bitter pill to swallow. No one at any time has given me a single reason for this PI versus PC status (Co-pilot vs. Pilot-in-Command). My experienced pilot friends here are convinced that it is all motivated by envy and jealousy. They constantly tell me, "Rich, if they didn't hold this back from you and let you be one of them, they would have absolutely nothing over you. You have flown and still fly aircraft that they will *never* fly, and they are insanely jealous."

I just can't relate to that kind of thinking. I was a young inexperienced pilot once, too. I looked up to older more experienced pilots; I hung on their every word! I still look up to other experienced aviators and I'm always grateful to learn. I think back to when I got hired by the airlines and how I looked up to the Captains, many who were older then than I am now. I knew one fact as it related to them—they knew more than I did, period. I didn't have to like them (although I usually did), but I knew in my heart and mind that I had much to learn from them. They had seen and done so much more year after year in the aviating world, this world in which I was still very new. I have to remind myself that with the exception of a few of the full-timers, the people here are reservists who do not fly for a living. Flying for a living is what I do know, pretty much *all* I know, professionally speaking. But you would never know it here. The disappointments just keep piling up.

Here is a story that illustrates how my flight experience was not considered of any value, and how what I had to offer was balked at, ignored, and avoided. It was a "dark and stormy night," and I was flying with First Lieutenant James Rookner, who was the Pilot in Command, and I was the PI. We were in the cockpit making preparations, but I was uneasy. Here's what I wrote later in my journal about this flight: "Well, fortunately, I did *not* have to fly last night. The weather was getting bad; isolated thunderstorms with wind forecasts of over 50 MPH. Rookner did a decent job on the decision-making process, but there I was, depending on a very low-time pilot to make the decision that affects *my life* and others."

Maybe I can help you understand why I felt that way by recounting our credentials. LT Rookner has more Black Hawk time and goggle time than I do by a few hundred hours. He has about 800 hours total time, with 600 hours of that in the UH-60 (Black Hawk). The extra 200 hours or so is some light plane training (he does not have his license in airplanes) and the primary helicopter trainer in Army flight school, mostly the TH-57 (like a Bell Jet Ranger). He has about 180 hours NVG (or Goggle Time). I believe he has been flying around seven years, and is about thirty years old. LT Rookner is a basic Army Aviator, what in Army aviation circles is referred to as having "slick wings," as they have no star *or* wreath on them. He has *never* been a full-time professional pilot, as he is a part-timer in the reserves. He has his commercial helicopter rating and helicopter instrument rating. In fairness, this is LT Rookner's second trip to the "sand box." I do value his knowledge as it relates to this country and this unit's mission there.

I have over 16,000 hours total time, of which 2,000 hours are in helicopters. My Black Hawk time is only about 300 hours, and my NVG (Goggle time) is around 75 hours, which are the only categories that my time is less than the young Rookner's. The helicopters I have flown are the UH-1H (Huey), the TH-55A (my primary Army trainer), and the OH-58A (flew in addition to Huey in one of my units—maintained currency with both at the same time). After I got out of the Army *the first time,* I flew for an offshore company flying the Bell 206, and Bell 206L-1 (Jet Ranger and Long Ranger—civilian helicopters) out to the oil rigs in the Gulf of Mexico. After returning to full-time active duty in the Army, I flew the OV-1B, C, and

D Mohawk (single pilot) twin turboprop airplane for eight years. I was also an instructor pilot in the Mohawk. I have flown the following jets: B-727, B-737, B-757, B-767, MD-80 (DC-9), DC-10, and the DA-2000 (Falcon 2000). Approximately 12,000 hours of my time has been making good decisions, especially as it relates to weather, the aircraft, and keeping the crew on the same page . . . flying these jets.

I have been a professional pilot for over thirty-five years, always a full-time pilot, never just a part-timer. I have been an airline pilot for one of the world's largest major airlines (eighteen years; retired at age fifty), and was a Captain there for eight years. I now fly private corporate/business jets. I have flown domestically all over the U.S., and internationally in Mexico, the Caribbean, Canada, Central America, South America, and Europe. I am a Master Army Aviator (star *and* wreath), and I am fifty-four years old. This is my one and only trip to the "sand box."

So with all that in mind, the most disturbing thing about that experience, with the bad weather, is that he made all of the decisions, and hardly included me in any part of it. He occasionally listened to me to be quasi-polite. He made all the phone calls and all the radio calls. He is less than a good communicator. He talks fast and sometimes mumbles, and very rarely makes a complete sentence or a clear point. As I said in my journal, he made the right decision to not fly; but my life was in his hands, so to speak. Well, not really, because I would never let him kill me with that helicopter. I don't care how ugly it would get or how condescending he became; he would have a fight on his hands if operating an aircraft in any condition that I don't believe is safe. (Within reason, of course, since we are in a combat zone, and nothing is really safe).

It is a shame that I have to view it like this. Instead of utilizing my experience, it is ignored and shunned. This Army Reserves unit is the loser here, and they are making me pretty miserable along the way. This is all more than humbling; it is insulting. Still, I am trying to do what the Bible commands, and do my job as if I'm doing it for God, to do all I do as unto the Lord. There will come a time when the Lord will honor His word. It may not be on this side of eternity, but He will bless me, I am certain. He already has blessed me by giving me the strength and moral courage to face this disappointing situation with dignity and honor. To God be the glory!

Let me give you an analogy. Let's suppose that you were a doctor the last thirty-five years of your life. You started out in one particular specialty, but have been practicing another one for the bulk of your career. You did some refresher training on your original specialty about five years ago, and have now been practicing both specialties since then. However, the clinic where you practice the original specialty has young inexperienced doctors, whom you work under. As a matter of fact, you don't even have approval to perform the job you once did twenty years ago due to inter-office politics. You are vastly more qualified than most doctors who work there. Wouldn't this scenario be sad? Even more sad if you volunteered to get re-qualified in this specialty to serve your country? How about to serve your country in combat? You could substitute almost any profession to fit this analogy and the results would be the same—a shame that a person is not being utilized to their full potential for ridiculous, petty reasons.

If I haven't convinced you that there is some resentment helping to create this situation against me, here's another piece of evidence. Every month the headquarters of our unit publishes a flight time sheet with all crewmembers on it; that's all pilots and back-seaters. It shows the crewmembers' total flight time, and specifics such as UH-60 (Black Hawk) time, and NVG (Night Vision Goggle) time, etc. Most people here have in the hundreds to a thousand hours, and a few have several thousand hours in the total time block. I have over sixteen thousand in the total time block. Well, I would have . . . but there's just one problem. My name is always *missing* from the form. I have inquired through our operations personnel at our base; they in turn have inquired to headquarters about it (who publishes the form), but never get a straight answer. They *are* logging my time as I *do* get individual flight time sheets, but the unit sheet on display for all personnel in our unit to see, and to use in order to prepare a "risk management form" prior to every flight, always has my name and data missing.

This is a task performed by PCs, and all of them now know my time. They used to ask me, "Wellington, how much time do you have? You're not on the form." I have heard some of the instructor pilots at headquarters say, "I'm not putting Wellington on the form; his flight time skews our records." I have also witnessed them turning in records to higher headquarters reflecting my time as only a couple of thousand hours total. Maybe they don't want higher headquarters to ask any embarrassing questions. Or, they are concerned about attention being drawn to someone other than themselves. They don't know I've seen them and heard them do and say these things. Instead of being happy for me, let alone proud that they have someone with that much experience, they hide it. All I can figure is that they are concerned that my time and experience takes away from their glory somehow.

Let me share one more story. I'll title this "A Typical Morning."

Well, it is Ground Hog Day number 317. I head out to the helicopter for the morning crew swap, preflight, and run-up. I depart my room at precisely 0650 (on *my* watch; more on that later) and head for the operations building, where my flight gear is hanging in a little cubby. I strap on the 9,000 pounds of junk that we must fly with. I put it on because there is no other way of carrying it all. I walk through Operations to let them know I'm heading that way. I get to the helicopter and pile my 9,000 pounds of junk on the ground. I begin my wait. I am there about five to ten minutes early—just the way I like to operate. I don't expect others to be early, but they should not be late. My watch (I said I'd mention it again) is always five minutes fast. I do everything early; I take being punctual very serious.

All the players are here for the crew swap; well, with the exception of my PC (Pilot in Command). I sarcastically ask: "Wonder what time the 0700 crew swap is going to take place?" Everyone just chuckles because they are all quite used to this person being late. If he has ever been on time, I truly don't remember it. This punctuality stuff is not his baby, but if it were, we would certainly hear about it. I've seen him arrive late for a real mission, but of course he blamed it on someone else, and his clock. One time he actually did not wake up for a crew swap, and he came down hard on everyone for not waking him up, overlooking the point that he was the main one at fault. He is not really into personal responsibility, unless he is talking about your personal responsibility. It doesn't matter though; he looks great in the eyes of this organization, and that is *all* that matters. Unfortunately for most of us, there are only a handful of individuals that look good in the eyes of this organization.

Well, here he comes at 0720. I have most of my checks and procedures accomplished and I am just about ready to put on the 9,000 pounds of junk and climb in for the run-up. I have to wait for him to catch up, however. Finally, he is ready and we run-up the aircraft. It feels much the same as when you fly with him; he does not know how to do this job and make it enjoyable. He is always waxing eloquent (mostly he mumbles) about what he wants to impart to you today from his vast experience of aviation knowledge. Maybe he can clear up for you one more time how he likes to enter a traffic pattern (heavy sarcasm added). If I can just glean some of that knowledge, I too could someday be condescending in the cockpit (more sarcasm). Of course, there is nothing I despise more; condescension in the cockpit does *not* work.

Finally, it is all done. Now it is time to head inside, prepare my intelligence report (which is always depressing), and attend the morning meeting. Another place where some people try to impart a vast amount of life knowledge on just about everything. In order to be generic, suffice it to say that the political climate over here stinks. It stinks in all directions: (1) in our team, (2) in our unit—which is even worse, and (3) in this country, Iraq, in general. I truly believe that the goals that the U.S. made with regard to Iraq have all been a dismal failure. I hope I am wrong, but I don't believe I am. If I am right, then thousands have lost their lives in vain, and a gazillion dollars has been wasted.

That's an example of a typical day over here. Mind you, I have not even included the miserable daily latrine/hygiene situation, the terrible food, the dirt, the heat, the smells, and so on. I've just discussed the preparation for the daily routine of duties. Along with this duty is the fact that all of this takes place almost exactly the same way each and every day. A fun and enjoyable job would be hard to handle every single day without breaks, and this is anything but fun and enjoyable. The highlight of the day is placing an "X" on the calendar, signifying that another day in this worthless prison sentence is complete. Like I said, it's been a major disappointment.

Now, I would like to say something in defense of the United States Army, its Reserves, and National Guard. This strife and resentment among the unit here is not indicative of what most Army Aviation units are about. This is not the norm. This unit has individuals that have been allowed to build their own little empire, and now it is hard to dismantle the force they've created. You will not be accepted here unless you are willing to recognize that *they* are better than you, that you know little to nothing, and that you will pay all your dues here, whether or not you paid years of them elsewhere. Without this realization up front; you will get nowhere here. I came into this reserve unit naively and honestly accepting and liking everyone. It took deploying with them to see their true colors. They are all about making themselves look good, and if you detract from that, you will feel the heat.

I really feel sorry for people like LT Rookner. He is purely a product of society. He prides himself on his tolerance and centrist position on just about everything, which really means that he believes in nothing, stands for nothing, and is free to waffle and change his opinion on everything. There is one exception to that tolerant outlook, however. He cannot find tolerance in his heart and mind for something as narrow-minded as Christianity, the Creation story, or set moral standards. He has all the tolerance in the world for anything and everything that is immoral, worldly, selfish, and self-serving. Again, I feel sorry for him.

One day one of the enlisted soldiers said to me, "Mr. W, you haven't been treated fairly here, sir. I respect you and enjoy flying with you." I thanked him for his kind remarks and assured him that I was OK. It gave me the opportunity to share that my mission here is to serve a Higher Power. The Bible states to do all we do "as unto the Lord," as I've said before. That is hard to do sometimes; yet, it's the right thing to do and it will also bring you peace.

* * * * * * *

It is time to turn all this around and put a positive spin on it. This experience makes me realize that I have led a pretty charmed life. In almost fourteen years serving as an active Army pilot, I never experienced the political, stab-each-other-in-the-back climate I've experienced here in deployment. As an airline pilot flying with true professionals, I also did not see a hint of that sort of thing among pilots. That's why I jumped into this tour so wide-eyed and so naively! It is also why I didn't detect it for so long, because it did not rear its ugly head until the deployment. It appears that a lot of these people are without moral standards, are very insecure, and basically unhappy with their lot in life.

I had to realize that there are people that resent you and will do you harm if given the opportunity. That was hard for me to accept because I just can't think like that. I had to realize that there are just as many enemies *inside* the wire as *outside* the wire. I had to quit being so transparent and open with them, and had to guard my feelings and interests. Lastly, I had to ask, "What would God have me do?" The Bible not only says to pray for those that spitefully use you, it also says to love your enemies. That is *very* hard to do.

There is something else I did that helped me release my anger and frustration. You can do it, too, and you will be the better person for it.

Read the Bible.

The stories in the Bible do more than entertain us. I believe that God gave us these stories so we can apply the lessons learned to our lives today. There are some amazing stories about people who were treated unfairly, and then how the situation turned around to their good! I'm going to share one of these stories and my personal interpretation of it. It is the story of Queen Esther.

The setting for the book of Esther is ancient Persia (the area of modern-day Iraq and Iran), which was the dominant kingdom in the Middle East during the fifth century B.C. The Jewish people had been taken captive decades earlier by the Babylonians, and many Jews remained there as exiles in Persia. Esther and her family were among this Jewish minority, living in the capital city of

Susa. The time frame was several hundred years B.C. I don't give an exact date, because different dates are argued by many historians. I'm not a theologian or a historian; however, I believe God gave us His word (the Bible) so we can all understand it, and that we don't have to be theologians to do so. I believe that this story is true and accurate. What you will read below is the "Richard Wellington paraphrased version" of the story of Esther.

****

The King was having a party. From the story I gather it was a heavy drinking party, and feeling loose, the King wanted to "show off his stuff." (See why I don't even pretend to be a theologian?) Anyway, one of the things he wanted to show off was his beautiful wife, the Queen, who was having her own party in another room. Who knows what she was thinking, because no one ever had the right to just shrug off a request from the King—not even the Queen. But shrug it off she did, refusing to go. She continued to have her party selling kitchen accessories, jewelry, and home décor products, and blew off the King's request (no disrespect intended; it's just humor). Well, this made the King more than a little angry. In a nut shell, the King decided he would be looking for a new Queen!

Well, fast-forward to what you may have guessed . . . Esther became that new queen! She was beautiful and she found great favor with the King and all the people. Esther was related to a man name Mordecai, who had raised Esther after her parents died when she was young. They were both Jews, and Esther became the new queen without the King knowing that she was Jewish. Mordecai had urged her to keep this fact to herself. One day Mordecai overheard a plot from some officials who had plans to kill the King. Mordecai related that news to Esther, and she informed the King, and the plot was thwarted. It was noted in the King's book of records that Mordecai was the person who uncovered this scheme, ultimately saving the King's life.

Meanwhile, the King had an official working for him named Haman. Imagine Haman as a typical modern-day politician that you do not like (putting it lightly). Haman was all about himself and power, but he had the King fooled and he remained in a seat of power and influence. The local populace would bow to Haman as he walked by, except for Mordecai. He refused to bow down to show Haman honor. This made Haman furious; so furious that after discovering that Mordecai was a Jew, he not only wanted to kill Mordecai but also wanted to completely eliminate the Jewish people. Haman came up with legislation, which the King signed off on, that would accomplish that very task. It basically encouraged people to take part in the elimination of the Jews, and would even be profitable for those who participated in this terrible event. There were decrees sent throughout the entire kingdom explaining that all the Jewish people were to be killed on a certain date, several months later.

Mordecai and all the Jewish people found out about this decree, and they were heartbroken and terrified, to say the least. Remember, the King still did not know that Esther, his wife and queen, was Jewish. Also, as was the custom in this kingdom, any law once decreed by the King could not be reversed. There seemed to be no hope for the Jewish people.

Mordecai eventually got through to Queen Esther that she must do something. He told her that she may be her people's only hope. This would be difficult to say the least. If anyone (including the Queen) approached the King's inner court uninvited, that person would be put to death. The only exception was if the King were to raise his royal scepter in approval of such an unannounced meeting. Nonetheless, this would be a risky position for Esther to put herself in, and it was still impossible for her to get the law reversed. Either way, Mordecai reminded her that she, too, was a Jew, and thus had no real protection from this decree. She must be in this position as the queen for this very moment in time. Esther agreed to approach the King, but first she asked Mordecai to have the Jewish people fast and pray for three days and nights.

The day came and Esther approached the King's inner court. The King, seeing his lovely Queen, raised the royal scepter approving the meeting. He essentially asked what he could do for her. She responded by inviting the King and Haman to attend a banquet. At this point the King was really probably shocked, chuckling inside as to what a frivolous request this was for the serious risk she took. Once Haman had news of it all, of course he was ecstatic to be invited!

The King and Haman arrived at the banquet, the King still a little puzzled as to what Queen Esther's intentions were. After he inquired, she told them that she wants them to attend a second banquet. I don't really understand why she couldn't have accomplished what she wanted at this one, but I'm sure she had her reasons. Maybe it was to make Haman more comfortable and vulnerable before unleashing her plan.

Haman was still angry and troubled about Mordecai. Following the advice from some of his friends and his wife, he built a set of gallows on which to hang Mordecai. He planned to make this request to the King to hang Mordecai the next time the King summoned him. Some versions describe the device of death as a gallows, and others as an impaling pole; both clearly instruments of death. The height of the device was quite high, in order to make a public spectacle out of Mordecai, or whoever was killed on this device.

That night the King could not sleep, so he ordered his staff to bring to him and read from the King's official book of records. As they did so, the story was read about Mordecai and his part in stopping the plot to kill the King. The King wanted to know what had been done to reward Mordecai; they responded that nothing had been done. By now it must have been morning and the King summoned Haman. He asked Haman something to the effect of: What should be done to honor a man whom the King wants to honor? Now, Haman was initially planning to ask the King about executing Mordecai at this meeting, so this question set him off guard, but quite pleasantly. Haman arrogantly thought that, of course, the King wanted to honor *him*. He rattled off all kinds of things, including robes, royal crests, and one of the King's horses to parade this "man of honor" around town with. Then, the King demanded that Haman bestow these honors on Mordecai! Well, Haman was even more furious, yet obviously had no choice but to comply with the King's orders. He would have to deal with Mordecai later.

The King and Haman then went to the second banquet. The King once again wanted to know what he could do for Queen Esther; just what her petition was. It was then that she revealed that her people were to be destroyed, that there was a plan made by someone to kill them all. The King was livid! He wanted to know who devised such a plan, and she pointed to Haman as the designer of this plot. The King was so enraged he went outside. Haman, knowing that he was in real trouble, fell across the couch where the Queen was, and begged for his life. When the King came back inside, he was even more furious. It appeared to him that Haman was even willing to assault the queen in the King's presence! One of the King's staff that knew about the gallows (made by Haman for Mordecai) pointed them out for all to see, as they were clearly in sight from where the banquet was being held. The King in his rage ordered Haman to be executed by the very instrument of death that Haman intended to use on Mordecai. Talk about an ironic twist!

Well, that wasn't the end of the story. The King allowed Esther and Mordecai to create another kingly decree that let the Jewish people defend themselves from any assailants. This didn't reverse the other law but at least countered it. When the day came, the Jewish people fought in self-defense and defeated all of their enemies. The King also gave Esther and Mordecai the entire estate that once belonged to Haman. Mordecai was given power and authority second only to the King. Queen Esther was the savior of her people, and to this day that event is celebrated by the Jewish people.

****

So, what can we learn? There have been times in my life that seemed impossible or hopeless, just as Mordecai and Esther must have felt. Times when there were "Hamans" who were totally against me. Times when things were so desperate that it wasn't worth trying. This story from the Bible helped me the most during my deployment. Even now, every time I think I have it all figured out and attempt to predict disaster or victory, I usually have it wrong. The story of Esther reminds me that God's ways aren't my ways, but that we can rest assured that God is sovereign.

My desire is to make sure that I belong to Him, and that He considers me to be His child, one of His people. No, I'm not Jewish, but the Scriptures tell me that believing in Jesus allows us Gentiles to be grafted into His family, much like adoption. The comfort portrayed in Esther's story is limitless. When all seems lost; when you see the enemy on every front; when something is so incredibly disappointing that you just don't know where the strength will come from to endure—I recommend reading the story of Esther.

Humor: When Flying Was Fun

I've flown quite a bit, both as a pilot and as a passenger. Including times as a kid, my flying experience spans over fifty years. Wow, have I seen some changes in this mode of travel!

For many years commercial flying was a lot of fun. These days it fills a need and gets a person from point A to point B, but can really be lacking in the fun department. Some of you reading this only know of the current twenty-first century travel experience. If that's the case, I hope this chapter brings you a little enlightenment and maybe a chuckle or two.

I'll never forget being a brand new Boeing 727 Flight Engineer in the mid-1980s. I could not have been any happier. To say that some of the Captains were a little eccentric could possibly be an understatement. Eccentric or not, they were men I looked up to. They knew their airplane and how to fly it. They showed up to training at the "school house" in a coat and tie. When pilots travelled, their families were the best dressed and the best behaved.

Here are a few brief memories I have from those days.

- One Captain had a life-sized rubber chicken in his flight bag. After landing and while taxiing in to the gate, he often opened his window and, leaning most of his body out of the aircraft, placed this rubber chicken under the windshield wiper of the jet. After arriving at the gate someone would always notice, and the fun would begin. He never tired of this little joke.
- Another Captain, who was really into restoring antique cars, brought on his trips a bag of hand tools and dirty old car parts, such as carburetors, to work on in his hotel room. (Can you imagine trying to explain that going through security in today's world?)
- A young boy around nine or ten years old came to the cockpit. He had been on our previous flight leg, and we had a few minutes on the ground before we were to depart again. Most people are amazed to see

the vast number of instruments, switches, circuit breakers, etc. The Captain thought this youngster would be duly impressed as well. While pointing out the myriad of old round dial type gauges, he told the young boy, "Look at all the clocks!" Surely the boy would say, "Wow, why do you need so many clocks?" or "That's a lot of clocks." Instead he said, "Captain, I noticed on the last leg at altitude feeling a slight burble. Were we approaching critical Mach speed, or was that just a little unstable air?" I was the co-pilot then, and I and the flight engineer burst into laughter, and asked "Captain Sky King" to point out a few more clocks.

Being an airline pilot in those days was the top of the heap in flying. The pay was great (after being there awhile), the schedule was great, and so was the retirement. It was a hard long road to become an airline pilot, and a very competitive one. Once there, you had "arrived"... you were "living the dream" literally. But in today's world of piloting, "living the dream" is a statement usually made with a dose of sarcasm. At many airlines today none of those statements about great pay, schedule, and benefits would be accurate. Before, it gave one a sense of pride to say that he or she worked for an airline. But airline flying today is embarrassing to those of us who remember the "good old days." Not to make bus travel look bad, but flying today often resembles traveling by bus. You find yourself in incredibly long lines to get through security, the agents at the gate can be less than friendly, and the seats could not be much more cramped and uncomfortable.

How did we get here, I ask? The 9-11 terrorist threat to use airplanes as weapons explains the security issues. Agree with it or not, security is here to stay. Aside from that, what has happened to the overall experience, the amenities, the meals (or lack of), and so on, that has changed so drastically over the past couple of decades? Many would agree with me when I call the airline industry a "Giant Race to the Bottom." I alluded to this earlier, but now will explain a little bit more.

There were only a couple of low-cost carriers at that time that were to survive. They were doing a good job but did not offer the same product as the major carriers. They did not really compete directly with the major carriers in most markets because they went to some cities where other airlines didn't want to go. They had their own niche, and like it or not, in their world they did a good job. Their employees were and in some cases still are well-compensated, and they work as a team—an attitude that comes from the top.

When the major carriers and low-cost carriers decided to compete head-to-head, that's when the giant race to the bottom began. The price to fly at the major airlines did come down, but it didn't always stay down and it could not be any more complicated of a structure. The salaries of the employees eventually came down, too, causing a very disgruntled workforce. There is one huge exception to this lower-wage issue and that is upper management. Their salaries have soared. Even if the company is on the brink of financial ruin, they will get their salaries and perks while the employees receive slick glossy mailings describing some new "benefit," which in actuality is always a reduction or an elimination of a benefit they always had. Don't try to blame it all on the unions either. The most successful low-cost carrier is highly unionized, and everyone is mostly happy with them, including their management, their employees, and customers.

What does the traveling public get? A hub-and-spoke system totally outdated along with unrealistic connections almost guaranteed to miss with any weather or air traffic control delays. What else does the traveling public get, since this race to the bottom has pretty much bottomed out? Little to no food, cramped seats, attitudes from many employees (understandable, but attitudes nonetheless), cramped terminals (not all of them), jet bridges not designed for the jets they use, baggage fees, not enough overhead space on some of the smaller jets and planes, and the list goes on, and on, and on.

However, some indirect responsibility lies with the traveling public. We, the traveling public, want to fly coast-to-coast at bus fares, when it really isn't possible. Oh, sometimes the airlines offer it at a losing proposition just to grab some customers; but in the long run, everyone loses. Remember: the only carriers now providing a consistent product, considered good by most folks, is the handful of lower cost carriers that did it right all along. Don't kid yourself though. They do not always offer low-cost fares, and my hat's off to them, as they still require themselves to make a profit to stay in business. The major airlines, on the other hand, stick mostly to what they've done in the last twenty years: debt to bankruptcy protection, to reorganization, to merging, to repeat over and over again. Along the way a name or two disappears and becomes a part of airline history. I took an airline management class in the early 1980s and the professor predicted that there would only be a handful of carriers in the market someday. I believe he was pretty much on target.

Where does humor fit in here, you may ask? Admittedly this discussion hasn't been very funny so far. But in today's airline world it is amazing what you'll see out there, and there's a lot of humorous sights. It's almost one notch away from allowing chickens and roosters to board. I observe that the "normal" traveling ensemble for many folks is shorts, a t-shirt, and flip-flops (and clean is not required). I personally would not go to the convenience store dressed like this. People spend thousands of their hard-earned dollars to travel around the world in this fashion— or lack of. Here are a few special things I've seen:

- people clipping their toe nails with their smelly foot on the seatback in front of them,
- incredibly dirty smelly people you have to sit next to for hours,
- families who refuse to offer any discipline to their children, who are irritating everyone around them,
- someone who kicked my seatback for hours,
- someone behind me reading the newspaper, opening it up so wide and pushing it out so far that he used my head to keep it propped up. (This happened to a friend of mine that eventually crushed the man's newspaper

and rolled it up in a little ball. Obviously this behavior is not uncommon.)

- And what about baggage? I've seen people try and put their bags in the space in front of *my* seat. I've seen people dragging bags just shy of the size of a footlocker on the plane, and then causing the flight to depart late because the bag had to be checked at the last minute.

- It would not be fair to talk of the shrinking size of the seats without also mentioning the growing size of a good bulk of the seats' inhabitants. Many times I have felt the oozing of the guest in the seat next to mine, overpowering my personal square footage. I actually had to be moved one time because the more than large person that bought the seat next to me should have purchased two seats.

None of these experiences happened while I was traveling free as an airline employee. No, these pleasures surfaced when I was in a completely different occupation, paying full fare, on business.

There is another phenomenon that goes with aviation like no other business category. Let me explain. In a hospital, I wouldn't start spouting off medical terms as if I knew a lot about medicine. I would talk humbly, ask questions, and listen intently when doctors or nurses offer their counsel or direction. But as a pilot, I have heard some interesting comments on planes.

- Departing a city where I know the person waxing eloquent doesn't have a clue as to the direction of takeoff, confidently tells me: "We are going to takeoff, turn left, and go get on the jet stream—they always do that on this route."
- I've heard: "I can tell we are about to land because I can feel the pilot speeding up."
- When I was an airline Captain, a passenger approached me at the door as he was disembarking. He said, "You shut one down, didn't you?"—implying that I had shut an engine down in flight. I responded, "No,

sir." He looked back at me and said, "Yes, you did" and walked away. Where do they get this knowledge? Video games? Movies? It baffles me.

- I've heard passengers explain in detail how the airplane is supplied its oxygen, without understanding one thing about the aircraft's pressurization system.

- I heard a passenger ask for oxygen (not for medical reasons), as you would ask for a drink of water.

- Pilots used to say, "We will be on the ground in a few minutes." My old airline recommended that we didn't say that, and I agree. When we land, I still want to be in my seat and not "on the ground."

- Here's one that an airline is guilty of (and it drives me nuts). While taxiing out, the Flight Attendant says: "We've been cleared for takeoff. Please make sure your seat belts are fastened." I want to scream, *"No we haven't!"* We are still on the taxiway several turns away from takeoff, and may not even be talking to tower yet. Flight attendants often do the same with "We've been cleared to land." When, no, technically we haven't. Why make stuff up that is totally inaccurate?

- And my personal favorite misnomer: the "layover"—what it is and what it isn't. A layover means that the crew is spending the night (laying over) before the next flight. The time between flights on one day is just time between a connection. I've given up on that one now, because some airlines even print the term "layover" to represent connection time between flights.

Let me wrap this up on a different note. The changes we've seen in the airline world are indicative of our society as a whole. Culture changes, styles change, and even words change their meanings. The sad part in all this is that many personal standards have changed, too; standards in behavior, politeness, and etiquette, and it's not getting better. It would not surprise me to see our medical services and the professions it offers change drastically with society's bent towards socialized medicine. The world keeps demanding more for less—in some cases it just wants it free—and nothing is ever free. Somebody pays for it; always.

As things change, I continue to wonder if there is anything that *doesn't* change; anything that can be counted on. What, then, is really genuine?

Sight Picture

Sight picture, what is that? A sight picture is what a pilot views primarily through the windshield in relationship to the ground or runway. Whatever a pilot sees through a plane windshield is always important. But the most important sight picture is when he or she is landing the plane. Let me explain.

Let's suppose we are about to land a jet and we are now descending through one thousand feet AGL (meaning "above ground level"). This is the time under most circumstances that we want to have established what we would call a stabilized approach. At this point we want to be fully configured for landing. The slats and flaps are extended and in their landing position, the landing gear is down and locked, a relatively low rate of descent is established and set, the power or throttles are set, and checklists are complete. All these elements produce a nice glide path at a somewhat constant angle to the intended point of touchdown.

When all those tasks are done, there is a certain "sight picture" that you see out the windshield. With thousands of landings under your belt that sight picture becomes the norm. When you see a sight picture that is strangely different from the norm, it is time for alarm. A normal sight picture is the product of definite procedures, not some arbitrary or random way of doing things. Years and years of experience by other pilots before me have come up with these procedures. Ignoring these established standards can prove to be irresponsible or downright deadly. Following established procedures that have been proven time and time again is the best method of flying jets.

Life can be that way, too. As we *search for the genuine*—the genuine way or method to handle adversity and live life well—we need an established procedure, a true north to line up with, a sight picture to lead us to a smooth landing. I believe there are some "established procedures" for life that, if followed, will give us this sight picture and produce the most success in life.

What does that kind of success look like? Is it the pursuit of a genuinely good education or career, genuine love, or genuine relationships? The kind of success I am talking about is not just good things, nor the absence of failure. It also shows us the ability to handle difficulties or the ability to persevere. This definition of success may not be what you are familiar with, but remember, I am talking about *genuine success*. I have shared a few of my accomplishments as well as many genuine trials through stories about my family, relationships, military service, and aviation career. All these stories have one thing in common: blessings from God provided all the good things, and my faith in God helped me get through all the tough things. They are stories about genuinely prospering in this life, or better yet, *dealing with the realities of life* and preparing for an eternity.

Eternity is something that is ahead of every one of us, whether that is reckoned with now or later. The problems or situations you may be up against in your life may be minor irritations or very serious challenges that are overwhelming. I don't guarantee that there are any easy fixes. But I can guarantee that there is One who cares, One who loves you; and if you let Him, One who will provide a peace that passes all understanding. *God can calm your heart even in the middle of a storm*. This "sight picture" of faith is not privileged information only for me or my like-minded believing friends. It's for anyone.

That said, I want to share with you the basis of my most important belief—faith in God. The foundation of my belief is the Bible, period. I make no apologies for that. So what follows is a very condensed A to Z, cover-to-cover version of the Bible's general message to all of us, . . . well, Richard Wellington's interpretation of it, that is. Before you get ready to point out inaccuracies in what I write, I want to make a disclaimer: *my* writing is not inerrant or infallible, but I believe that God's word, the Bible, *is* inerrant and true in all respects. What I am attempting to do here is make some sense out of it all by giving a descriptive summary of what I believe the Bible is about.

I am not doing this in a scholarly way or with any attempt to sound like a theologian. I don't believe that God gave us His word to be understood by only theologians, scholars, priests, or preachers. I also don't think it is hard to understand. Yet, you have to be willing to read it from cover to cover, or I don't believe you will ever understand its contents completely. You don't need my description or summary either to help you understand it. You can go pick up the Bible and start reading it right now. It is my belief that God wants to speak to you and me through His word. You *can* choose to believe that the Bible is not true. I think that is a tragic belief, but it is direction you can go and one that God allows you to take.

Everything I am going to say is from my viewpoint, with the most fundamental of all my beliefs being that I truly believe the Bible is God's word to mankind. So, without further ado, here is Richard Wellington's summary of the Bible's message, and my reasons for why the Bible, God's word, is my operator's manual for a genuine life.

****

The Bible starts with the creation story: "In the beginning, God created the heavens and the earth" (Genesis, chapter 1, verse 1). Now, God has no beginning and no end. It is not easy for us to think of something eternal as being in the *past*. Most of us can somewhat grasp eternity in the *forward looking* direction. But God is in the past and in the future as well. He is out of time. He always was and always will be, period. You may ask, "Where did that assumption come from?" It is stated in many places and many ways throughout the Bible.

God created the world and everything in it, literally. The earth, the solar system, the plants, the animals—God created everything. It did not just happen or evolve on its own. He created man from dust and He created woman from man. The Bible says that human beings are created in God's image. The first two human beings were named Adam and Eve. They were created perfect and sinless, and were in perfect communion/relationship with God. He gave them a free will, so they would be free to choose. He placed them in a garden, saying they could eat of anything in the garden except from one particular tree. At that time there was no sickness, no death, and no agonizing toil with tending to the garden. All of the difficulties that we now experience in life did not exist yet. It was a perfect world. However, Adam and Eve chose to disobey God and eat of the forbidden tree and its fruit. At that moment, life for Adam and Eve and all their descendants of humankind became difficult. The world was no longer perfect. They fell out of fellowship or communion with God, and sin entered the world.

Everything changed. Work was more difficult, sickness and death entered the scene, and Adam and Eve were no longer in fellowship with a perfect, sinless, eternal God. They were embarrassed when God came looking for them, and for the first time they realized their nakedness and were ashamed. They tried covering themselves with leaves, but that was not good enough. God made them tunics of skin (an animal was killed as the first sacrifice) to cover their bodies as well as their shame. A sacrifice of blood by an innocent animal was made because of their sins. Adam and Eve's family multiplied on earth; and so began the history of mankind as God had planned, but one out of fellowship with Him.

As time went by, people grew more selfish and evil; so evil that God regretted creating the human race and decided to destroy the world with a great a flood. God showed favor to one particular man of faith and his family. This man's name was

Noah. God instructed Noah to build an ark—a huge boat/barn that would enable Noah and his family and the animal kingdom to survive this worldwide flood. You probably know the rest of the story, and for the sake of brevity, suffice it to say that the devastating floods came and covered the earth. Noah survived and the human race started over. (Please don't interpret the brevity of my retelling here to mean it was not important. The flood was a real, literal worldwide flood.)

Once again the human race grew in number, and once again, they became increasingly evil. Mankind's attempt to be like God or to exalt himself was next manifested in the building of a tower—the tower of Babel. Up until this point the whole earth had one language or one speech. God did not favor people's pride or self-reliance, so He confused their languages and scattered them throughout the world with different languages.

After this, one of Noah's descendants was named Abram (whose name would later be changed to *Abraham*). God made a covenant, an agreement, with Abraham, and chose Abraham's descendants to be God's chosen people. Through these people

God would eventually provide a Savior, and a way of redemption for humanity's fallen, sinful nature, so that fellowship with God could be restored. This was the origin of the Jewish race, also known as the Hebrews or the Israelites; God's chosen people.

A few generations later, one of Abraham's descendants named Joseph was sold by his jealous and hateful brothers as a slave into Egypt. God showed great favor to Joseph, and in due time Joseph had a powerful position in the land of Egypt. When famine came, the Hebrews relocated to Egypt and settled there. As the Hebrews became great in number, the powerful Pharaoh of Egypt made the Jewish people slaves. After four hundred years of bondage, God delivered His people out of the land of Egypt through one of His servants, Moses. The story of deliverance through the Red Sea is a *huge* part of the history of the Jews. It shows God's love and plans for them as a people. They were and still are God's chosen people, through whom One would come to correct the broken relationship with God and man, which had been lost in the Garden of Eden.

This deliverance of the Israelites from bondage was no quick affair, but it set the tone for how God wanted to bless them and make them a great nation. Starting with the days of Moses, God gave the people His commandments and instructions on how to live and how to worship. One of the aspects of this worship was sacrifice. Sin had to be paid for with a blood sacrifice. Remember when God sacrificed an animal for skins to cover Adam and Eve for their sin? Due to the awful nature of sin, it required the shedding of blood to be atoned for, or forgiven. Without going into too much detail, it was something that the priest would perform to atone or make amends for sin, in a temporary sort of way. These sacrifices would be animal sacrifices, often a lamb. The sacrificial lamb would be one without blemish. The lamb had done no wrong, but would be the substitute for the one who had sinned. Remember this point, as it was an important *foreshadowing* of what was to come centuries later!

The commandments God gave Moses to proclaim to His people were simple and straightforward, and what we refer to as the Ten Commandments. This was once again part of God's covenant with His people. Another aspect of this covenant was that God would give His people a *land of promise*—Canaan—a wonderful place to call home that would be theirs. Even after seeing numerous mind-boggling miracles right before their very eyes, the Israelites started to doubt that they were ever going to reach the land of promise. They started complaining and even wanted to go back to Egypt, where they had been slaves! Even worse, the Israelites started worshipping false Gods. Idolatry was something God would not tolerate then, nor will He tolerate it now. They angered God greatly and caused an entire generation to *not* see the land of promise.

After many years of wandering in the desert, a generation later, God gave the Israelites their land. All was well, until the story takes the turn you may expect. The Israelites turned from God and broke their part of the covenant or agreement/contract. God is very longsuffering, forgiving, patient, and loving, but He is also holy and must judge and correct and discipline.

I must say again that the brevity of this A-to-Z Bible summary is not intended to be the end-all guide at all, but simply a summary. It is my belief that it can help someone see the continuity of the message of the Bible; that it does in fact make sense from cover to cover, as a book with a literal beginning and an end.

Next, God's people experienced cycles: generations of blessings, followed by generations of destructive consequences when they turned from God. The analogy of God as a loving parent here is very appropriate. A large part of the Old Testament gives an account of God's people conquering lands and being blessed, and then the opposite, *being* conquered and facing certain destruction. However, with the destruction God always spared a certain group, a remnant of the faithful, to continue the lineage and blessing of His people.

Also in the Old Testament, not always in chronological order, are stories of people that ushered in the lineage of God's son, the Messiah, Jesus. There are books of the Bible containing wisdom in songs (the Psalms) and wise advice/sayings (Proverbs). Many of the psalms were written by King David, a very prominent figure in the Bible, who began his story as the shepherd boy who defeated the giant known as Goliath. Many of the proverbs and other writings of this nature were written by King Solomon, one of David's sons. The Bible claims that "all Scripture is God-breathed" (2 Timothy 3:16). The different books were written by men, yes; but men who were inspired and directed by the Holy Spirit of God. That's why I keep referring to it as *God's* word.

Besides the history of God's people and books of wisdom, poetry, and songs, there are many books of prophecy in the Old Testament. These books of prophecy foretell the coming of the Messiah, the Christ (Jesus), as well as prophecy of the end times, which has not all happened yet. What is truly amazing to me is that the Bible proves time and time again to be completely accurate. Prophecies or predictions hundreds of years before the events took place happened exactly as they were prophesied. Even in today's world of instant communication and information it would be impossible to create a hoax of this enormity. Some of these prophecies were written centuries before they happened.

No matter what the scoffers say, the Bible is completely accurate in all its prophetic writings. Due to all the events that have accurately come true already, I have no reason to believe that future events won't happen as the Bible predicts/prophesies as well. Don't take my word for it. Read them and prove it for yourself. Don't forget to read stories and events in their entirety. Do not take a sentence here or a sentence there, and take it out of context. Give it all an honest and fair evaluation.

The Old Testament ends with the book of Malachi, and the nation of Israel had finally returned to their homeland. This happened after their long captivity with the Babylonian Empire was over, and after their temple and form of worship had been restored. Between the Old and New Testaments of the Bible there is a period sometimes referred to as the "silent years" of approximately four hundred years.

So in a nutshell, the Old Testament is a collection of books about God and His creation, specifically the creation of mankind in God's image. The first humans were to have dominion over all the earth, but chose to disobey God and fell out of fellowship with God. After the flood that almost destroyed the human race, God in His mercy chose the Hebrews to be His people. We read all about the history of His people and His plans for them, which was ultimately to restore fellowship between God and human beings. Additionally there are books of instruction and wisdom, songs of inspiration, and prophetic books during the Jewish captivity in Babylon that offer hope of restoration and details of the Messiah to come.

Well, this is a *very* condensed version of the Old Testament, to say the least. However, I do it this way in order to prove that there is continuity from the Bible's beginning to its end. There is an overarching theme, a plan. In my opinion, it is a plan that not only proves itself with the past but also with the remainder of what *will* come to pass. Over and over, the Bible has been proven to be a reliable and accurate document. Now, let's see how the rest of the Bible fits into that overall plan.

****

The setting of the New Testament is the time when Rome was the dominant world power. The Jewish people once again followed their traditions and customs according to the Law of Moses (also referred to as Mosaic Law), but they were under the authority and thumb of the Roman Empire. Jesus was born into this setting, at a time when his people were oppressed by a foreign power yet again.

As the New Testament opens, we read the long Jewish lineage of Jesus, all the way from Abraham and King David. Then the angelic announcement is made to Jesus' parents, and the story is told of the simple birth of Jesus. Of course, now we refer to this as the Christmas story. You may not know it, but the story of Jesus fulfilled many prophecies one hundred percent accurately.

Again, it is not my desire to sound like a theologian here, as I am not. But the list of prophesied events that took place—before, during, and after the life of Jesus on this earth—were nothing short of astounding! One of the prophecies that came true was that He would be born of a virgin, by God's Holy Spirit. God was His Father. He had a stepfather, Joseph, and his mother was

Mary, who had not had relations with Joseph. This virgin birth is very important, not only because it was prophesied in the Old Testament but also because it made Jesus truly the Son of God. He was all man, but also all God. Granted, this is a very hard concept to understand, but it is a very important point.

The first books of the New Testament are called the *Gospels*, a term that means "good news." The Gospels are Matthew, Mark, Luke, and John. The Gospels give us the stories and teachings of the life of Jesus. The accounts are told by different individuals from different perspectives. Many people today looking for a reason to claim that the Bible contradicts itself, sight the differences of the Gospel accounts as their proof. The stories are just examples of how different people view and report the same events differently. Reporting from their own personal perspective does not contradict the other accounts.

Each Gospel book accurately reflects that Jesus was and is the sinless Son of God, and that He died on a cross, and that He was raised from the dead. They record his teaching and sermons, as well as show his relationship with his followers, the twelve disciples. The Gospels show that Jesus was clear of his purpose and mission: to seek and to save sinners who were lost. He died for all of our sins as the sinless, perfect sacrifice for sins. Remember the Old Testament's foreshadowing of the payment that was needed for sin, in order for our holy loving God to forgive? From the time Adam had sinned in the Garden of Eden, a spotless animal's blood had to be shed for the remission of sins and to atone for sin. Jesus Christ put an end to that system of sacrifice once and for all, because he was the *perfect, spotless Lamb of God,* who made the final payment for our sins.

The Gospels record exciting accounts of miracles Jesus performed—healing the lame, feeding thousands of people, even raising the dead. He performed these miracles to give glory to His Father. Jesus was really cool! I don't mean that with any disrespect or say it flippantly. We learn so much about Jesus in these New Testament books, and hence, about the nature of God.

Sadly, Jesus own people as a majority did not accept Him. The Jewish religious leaders of the day felt threatened and constantly tried to trip Jesus up or catch him breaking the Law of Moses. Of course they couldn't, so they accused Him falsely and set out to have Him killed. Jesus called them "snakes and vipers" and often displayed His disdain for hypocritical religion. In addition, Jesus gives us some signs to watch for that will usher in the end times. Many translations of the New Testament show the words of Jesus in red print. I find this to be a very helpful tool in my study of the scriptures.

Following the four Gospels is the book of Acts (the Acts of the Apostles) that describes the formation of the church and the actions and teaching of many of the apostles. I might point out that the church is never portrayed as a *building*, but rather the church is *people*. The church is all those who choose to believe and follow the teachings of Jesus; to accept Him as God the Son, their Savior. This early church of Jesus' followers was empowered by God's Holy Spirit, and it spread quickly.

Next is a series of books, called epistles, which are letters to individuals and people groups of the newly formed churches. This newly formed church of Christ-followers consisted of both Jewish (Hebrew) and non-Jewish (Gentile) groups. The vast majority of these letters were written by the Apostle Paul who, prior to his conversion to Christianity, persecuted the new believers know as *Christians*. If there was ever an example of how God can turn someone's life around, it is the story of Paul. (I urge you to read his story in Acts.) These letters largely deal with how the church should conduct itself in worship, how it should care for one another, and deal with the world around them. If you want a "how-to" book for how to live, this section of the New Testament is it. It offers real answers for living that are not limited to time and/or culture.

Lastly, there is the book of Revelation, recorded by the apostle John while he was in exile. He wrote about his vision of Jesus and His return, about heaven, and about the events that will lead up to the end of the world as we know it today.

So there you have it. The Bible's message from A to Z. From beginning to end it is a story of God's love: "For God so loved the world that He gave His only begotten Son, that whoever believes

in Him should not perish but have everlasting life"
(John 3:16).

****

Remember when I struggled with huge disappointments during my military deployment and flying career? We all have tough times and enemies to deal with. Let God order your steps and your responses. Read His word, then fasten your seatbelt and wait to see what God will do. He will amaze you. He will give you strength to endure. He will give you a heart that actually feels sympathy for those trying to persecute you (which sometimes can be a huge miracle in itself). And He will teach you to wait, as in *wait on God.* Don't try and predict, manipulate, or affect the outcome in any way. Leave it totally up to God. Take the scriptures to heart and pray for those who spitefully use you! Love your enemies, as Jesus said. Try to be at peace with them. This does not mean you have to compromise your beliefs, but pray about whatever situation you are facing, and thank God in advance for whatever the outcome will be.

The Bible is filled with promises for God's people. Christianity is a *relationship* with God through the risen Son Jesus! It is not a book of rules. All through the Gospels Jesus teaches us how to live and sets an example for us. As Christians we don't conform to ritualistic dos and don'ts. But after we invite Him into our lives to be our Savior, and repent of our pride and sin, we try to live by Jesus' example—out of our love and appreciation for what He has done for us. That is the exciting part, and the part that we can *genuinely* apply to our lives for victory and success in all that we do.

Having Jesus Christ in your life also ensures that heaven is your eternal home. In the grand scheme of things that's pretty important. This earthly existence is nothing but a speck in comparison to all of eternity. Does that truth help you face your current problems, crushing disappointments, financial disaster, or relationship issues? Well, it gives us some perspective anyway. In reality, we all have issues and challenges here and now. But I firmly believe that we can handle them *all* a hundred percent better if we allow God to direct us so we can live with His plan in mind. His plan is always better than ours.

How much better it is to face this world with the Creator Himself on your side, as *your* heavenly Father. This is a life of faith. It must start with the understanding and acceptance of God's word. I strongly urge you to read God's word for yourself. Read some each day from both the Old and New Testaments. Read methodically, read often, and ask God to illuminate His word to you. I suggest reading an easy reading translation initially (for example, the *New Living Translation*). It is clear and written with today's language in mind. The Bible is "alive" with truth, and can speak to you as nothing else can.

Who is God's word for? It is for all of humanity, period. It is for all of us, *individually*. The word of God is for the successful, the hurting, those who seem to be winning in life, and for those who have lost everything. Is it something mystical or magical that will make everything in your life perfect? Absolutely not, but it is truth; the *genuine truth*.

There is so much in life that is not truth. The world is looking to feel good all the time, whether it is merely an "eat drink and be merry" philosophy or something lustful or even evil. We are living in a society where so much good is called bad, and so much bad is called good. Some people look to the government to fix all their woes. The government cannot do this and does not have the resources to so. There is nothing—absolutely nothing—*genuine* about this approach to life.

Ever heard an explanation of how a diamond is formed? Miles below the earth's surface, there are coal deposits under severe and intense heat and pressure for years. This heat and pressure is what turns that coal into a priceless diamond—a *genuine* diamond. There's nothing quick or easy about the process, but not much more beautiful when the process is complete.

I'm no geologist any more than I'm a theologian, but I can understand and make this analogy. God has planned pressure and heat for your life, not to make your life miserable but to make you the genuine article—the *genuine person* He has created you to be. Life is a pressure cooker.

We can't run from all of life's pressures and continue to mature and to grow in God's favor and blessing. We must stand the heat, knowing that it will bring a beautiful result! He has given us His word, the Bible, to believe and stand on in times of great peril and in times of success. Often it's in the moments of success that we feel no need for God. I know personally that I've made some of my greatest blunders in times of success with this wrong way of thinking.

What is genuine in life? What has always been genuine? God himself. It's a beautiful mystery that will unfold in your life if you will learn to fall in love with God's word. When you find what His word says to be true, then you will find life— genuine life.

Epilogue

It's 5:30 in the morning and I'm up early to take our dog out for a walk. Little Madeline, our miniature poodle dog, is my baby girl. She always brings me joy; as I always say, "She loves to be loved." Taking her for a walk is something I do pretty much every morning. The days of flying jets and helicopters are over, just a fond memory. As I walk through the streets of downtown San Antonio, I think about how thankful I am for the life I've lived, and for the one I'm now living.

When I get back to our downtown condo, I will make the coffee so it will be ready when Marie wakes. Sitting on the balcony of our home outside in the morning enjoying coffee is one of our favorite events of the day. We both share a Bible verse or two, and pray for those who are on our prayer list. We pray for and talk of our two grown sons, Rich and Jack, who now have families of their own.

Rich is a successful attorney, and Jack is quite the acclaimed studio musician, specializing in cello and bass guitar. We are excited because they are all coming to visit soon, since it is almost Christmas. It has been awhile since we have seen them, their wives, and their boys—you guessed it— Richie (Richard IV) and Jack Jr.

I thank God that He never allowed me to give up when things were really difficult. Believe it or not, I thank Him for the trials and disappointments of life, too. Right now, I thank Him mostly for Marie. "Who can find a virtuous wife?" the writer in Proverbs asks. "For her worth is far above rubies. The heart of her husband safely trusts her; so he will have no lack of gain" (Proverbs 31:10-11). She is truly my greatest blessing on earth, and I love her more than I can describe.

Yes, it's Christmas time in Texas at the Wellington house, and I could not be any happier. As I reach out and grab Marie's hand the love I feel for her is overwhelming. As I pray my voice cracks with the emotion of gratitude flooding my mind. My whole being is filled with genuine joy, peace, and love.

Printed in Great Britain
by Amazon